SWARM

PROJECT VENOM

STRIPES PUBLISHING
An imprint of Little Tiger Press
1 The Coda Centre, 189 Munster Road,
London SW6 6AW

A paperback original
First published in Great Britain in 2014

Text copyright © Simon Cheshire, 2014
Cover illustration copyright © Peter Minister, Jerry Pyke, 2014
Cover background and inside imagery courtesy of www.shutterstock.com

ISBN: 978-1-84715-438-5

A CIP catalogue record for this book is available
from the British Library.

Printed and bound in the UK.

10 9 8 7 6 5 4 3 2 1

SWARM
PROJECT VENOM

SIMON CHESHIRE

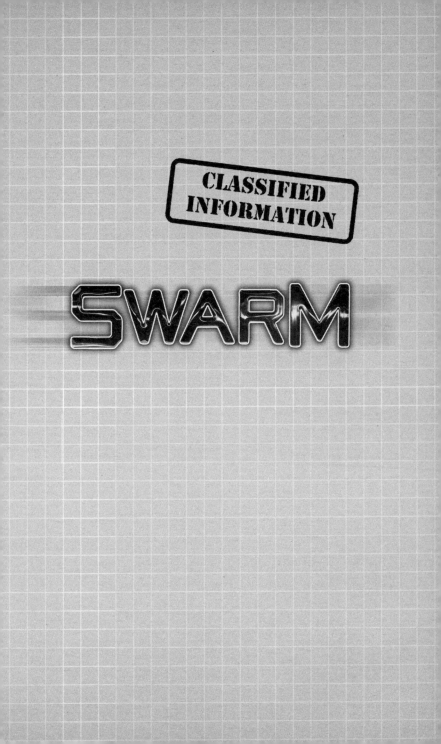

DEPARTMENT OF MICRO-ROBOTIC INTELLIGENCE

SPECIALISTS IN NANOTECHNOLOGY AMD BIOMIMICRY

HEAD OF DEPARTMENT

Beatrice Maynard: Code name QUEEN BEE

HUMAN OPERATIVES

Prof. Thomas Miller: TECHNICIAN
Alfred Berners: PROGRAMMER
Simon Turing: DATA ANALYST

SWARM OPERATIVES

WIDOW

DIVISION: Spider
LENGTH: 1.5 cm
WEIGHT: 1 gram
FEATURES:
- 360° vision and recording function
- Produces silk threads and webs stronger than steel
- Extremely venomous bite
- Can walk on any surface – horizontal, vertical or upside down

CHOPPER

DIVISION: Dragonfly
LENGTH: 12 cm
WEIGHT: 0.8 grams
FEATURES:
- Telescopic vision with zoom, scanning and recording functions
- Night vision and thermal imaging abilities
- High-speed flight with super control and rapid directional change

NERO

DIVISION: Scorpion
LENGTH: 12 cm
WEIGHT: 30 grams
FEATURES:

- Strong, impact-resistant exoskeleton
- Pincers to grab and hold, with high dexterity
- Venomous sting in tail
- Capable of high-speed attack movements

SABRE

DIVISION: Mosquito
LENGTH: 2 cm
WEIGHT: 2.5 milligrams
FEATURES:

- Long proboscis (mouthparts) for extracting DNA and injecting tracking technology and liquids to cause paralysis or memory loss
- Specialist in stealth movement without detection
- Capable of recording low frequency, low-volume sound

HERCULES

DIVISION: Stag beetle
LENGTH: 5 cm
WEIGHT: 50 grams
FEATURES:

- Extra-tough membrane on wing shells to withstand extreme force and pressure
- Serrated claw for sawing through any material
- Can lay surveillance 'eggs' for tracking and data analysis

MORPH

DIVISION: Centipede
LENGTH: 5 cm (10 cm when fully extended)
WEIGHT: 100 milligrams
FEATURES:

- Flexible, gelatinous body with super-strong grip
- Ability to dig and burrow
- Laser-mapping sensory functions

SIRENA

DIVISION: Butterfly
LENGTH: 7 cm
WEIGHT: 0.3 grams
FEATURES:

- Uses beauty rather than stealth for protection
- Expert in reconnaissance missions – can gather environmental data through high-sensitivity antennae

CHAPTER ONE

London. 3 September, 3 a.m.

From above, the lights of the city looked like a concentrated cluster of stars. Towards the west, where the cluster began to thin out, the street lights glowed a hazy yellow along the main road. Even in the early hours of the morning, a few cars sped along. Their tyres hissed against the road, damp and shining from a recent shower of rain.

Set back from the road was a large, rectangular building. It was plain and grey – just like the other factories and office blocks in the area. But this building was surrounded by a high metal fence.

The fence looked like it was made from ordinary steel, but it was actually constructed from the latest in smart materials, designed to register even the slightest touch. Alarms would trigger if anyone tried to climb or cut it. At a gate close to the building's main entrance, a security guard sipped a mug of tea in his brightly lit cabin. Across the gate was a swirly silver logo and the words:

SMITH-NEUTALL BIO LABS LTD.
NO UNAUTHORIZED ENTRY.
NO ADMITTANCE WITHOUT BIOMETRIC ID.
TRESPASSERS WILL BE PROSECUTED.

High above, a dragonfly zipped over the gate and headed for the building. Held in its thin legs was a scorpion. Close behind the dragonfly came a butterfly, carrying a curled-up centipede, then a stag beetle and a tiny buzzing mosquito. Meanwhile, a small spider had shot a line of web at the guard's hut, and was swinging in a wide arc up and over the fence, carried along on the chilly night breeze.

The sight of seven insects making their way towards a heavily guarded building would have been strange enough at the best of times. However, the truth about these insects was even stranger. All seven were miniature robots, each one an agent of the top-secret security organization, SWARM, otherwise known as the Department of Micro-robotic Intelligence. The dragonfly, its iridescent wings shimmering in the glow from the street lights, was code-named Chopper. The scorpion he was carrying was called Nero. Sabre the mosquito and Hercules the stag beetle brought up the rear, monitoring for signs that the robots had been followed or detected.

"We'll enter through the exhaust vents on the roof." Chopper's voice registered in the computer brains of his companions.

"Do you have a tight hold on me?" said the coiled centipede. His code name was Morph.

"Don't worry," said the butterfly, Sirena. "I've got you. We're nearly there."

The spider stayed silent. She usually did. Her code name was Widow, and the micro-fibre threads she spun were stronger than steel. She zipped up on to the flat roof of the building ahead of the others.

Chopper and Sirena landed beside a large metal vent, which ended in a flat grille, and Nero and Morph scuttled free. Sabre and Hercules maintained surveillance.

Chopper examined the closed grille using his night vision. "Entrance blocked," he said. "Morph, bottom-left corner shows a gap of 0.8 millimetres."

"Logged," replied Morph. The centipede scurried over. The flexible, gelatinous material of his body allowed him to squeeze through the tiny gap. Inside, he reformed into his normal shape. He found the mechanism and opened the grille, gripping it tightly with his tail. The others quickly entered and Morph let it close behind them.

"Our target could be anywhere in this building," said Chopper. "Mission priority is to locate any high-security storage bays and search them. The target is likely to be small and well hidden. Morph, take over surveillance, watch for movement up here. We must make sure that our exit route is clear. The rest of you, follow me."

Six miniature robots made their way down the ventilation pipe. They met a succession of mesh filters – Hercules the stag beetle cut each one using his serrated claw. After descending for several metres, they entered a high-tech chemistry lab.

The only light came from the distant street lights visible through the broad, bullet-proof windows. Within the room, LEDs blinked red and green on various pieces of equipment. Plastic biohazard suits were dangling on hooks beside signs:

STAY ALERT!
CARELESSNESS KILLS!

CONTAMINATION DANGER:
ENSURE YOU HAVE AN ALL-CLEAN
CONFIRMED ON ENTERING
AND LEAVING.

Chopper sent a coded transmission back to SWARM headquarters: "Hive 1 to SWARM."

SWARM's human leader, Beatrice Maynard, code-named Queen Bee, replied instantly.

"I hear you, Chopper, go ahead."

"We're in, Queen Bee," said Chopper. "Operation commencing."

"Begin recording," said Queen Bee. "And be careful."

"Logged, Queen Bee," said Chopper. He scanned the room. Data and images appeared back at HQ on the monitors in front of Queen Bee.

"The target's not here," said Sirena, whose antennae contained SWARM's most sensitive environmental data-gathering systems. "They run tests and experiments in this lab, but there's no secure storage."

"Hack into their computer system, see what you can find," said Chopper.

"Logged," said Sirena. She fluttered to the nearest PC.

Nero hurried over to the laboratory's airtight metal door to unlock it and gain them access to the rest of the building. Tiny probes flicked out from his pincers. They burrowed into a keycode panel. Seconds later, the panel bleeped and the door clunked as it unlocked and opened.

The robots moved out into the corridor beyond. Nero resealed the lab behind them.

"Human twelve metres south," said Chopper.

The robots kept to the shadows. A security guard wandered past the end of the corridor, whistling quietly to himself. Motion-sensitive lights in the walls blinked on as he approached, and off as he went on his way.

"We're too small to set those off," said Chopper.

"But not so small that we can ignore the laser grid," said Hercules.

Halfway down the corridor, a thin line of red light circled the walls, ceiling and floor. The beams emitted from it were invisible to humans, but the robots saw them as a flat, moving grid. Each laser beam was powerful enough to slice through them instantly.

"This grid guards the lab," said Chopper. "There are probably more outside the other restricted areas."

They watched the grid shifting back and forth for a moment. No human could have calculated a way through it, but within seconds the robots began to dart and jump. They timed their movements precisely, twisting in mid-air to avoid the beams, and landed safely on the other side.

Slowly, they made their way around the building, working downwards from floor to floor. Between them, they recorded every detail of the place.

Nero made a thorough scan of electrical systems. "I'm getting readings of high power usage in the basement," said Nero. "I suspect the bio-storage for holding live viruses and other dangerous substances is down there."

A laser grid outside the basement entrance confirmed that there was something important in there. The robots scuttled and darted past the grid, avoiding the deadly beams once more.

"Coded alarm system detected in vault door," said Chopper. "Hercules, bypass defences."

The beetle's dark carbon-fibre body would have been invisible to the human eye in the gloom. He scurried up the wall and cut into a small hatch above the basement's entrance. The others swiftly followed him. They crawled into a pipe used for running cables, and moved along it until they reached the room itself.

The vault they looked out on to was low and narrow. Walls, floor and ceiling were all polished metal. At the back was a large glass case labelled with a sign:

The case was filled with rows of coloured bottles and cylinders.

"Nero," said Chopper, "cut a tiny hole in the glass, on the side of the case where it won't be noticed. Sabre, go inside and confirm the target."

"Wait!" said Nero. "I can detect electrical activity in the floor. The area between us and the glass case is sensitive to touch. If it's triggered, the alarm will go off."

"We were small enough not to activate the corridor lights," said Chopper.

"This is different," said Nero. "I'm picking up readings from pressure pads all over the room. If even one of us lands on any connected surface, the alarm will trip. We're very slightly heavier than real insects. The difference is tiny, but it's enough."

"Is the glass case itself wired up?" said Chopper.

"Scanning," said Nero. "No, it isn't."

Widow scuttled forward. Taking careful aim, she fired a thread at the glass case, which stuck neatly at its exact centre.

"A zip line," she said quietly.

Hanging beneath the line by his pincers, Nero slid across to the case. The grippers in his feet engaged with the vertical glass and held him firmly in place. He scuttled around to the side of the case, a miniaturized cutter emerging from a tiny hatch in one pincer, a small suction cup from the other.

He carved a circle in the glass with the cutter, and pulled it free using the suction cup. Then he hurried back along Widow's thread, dangling by his legs.

Sabre buzzed across to the case, keeping well clear of the metal surfaces all around him. Folding back his mechanical wings, he wriggled through the hole.

"Anything?" transmitted Chopper.

Sabre's needle-like proboscis jutted forward from his mechanical mouthparts. One by one he directed wireless high-frequency probes towards the many glass bottles and Petri dishes around him. "There are various things here. These dishes contain live cell cultures of bacteria, viruses, or other disease pathogens. Some are highly toxic to organic life."

He crawled around the different bottles, each of them covered in printed and handwritten labels, his proboscis scanning and analyzing. At last, he approached a small glass phial, set apart from the others. It contained a red liquid that emitted a slight glow. Unlike the others, this container was not marked in any way.

"I've found it," he said.

Chopper signalled SWARM headquarters. "Target located, Queen Bee,"

"Good work," said the voice of Queen Bee. "Sabre, what's your analysis?"

Sabre's sensors processed the data he'd gathered. "It's a mixture of extracted DNA, viral organisms and poisonous chemicals.

Its molecular structure suggests that it affects mammals, birds and fish, some insect species and some reptiles. It kills almost instantly, either by contact or inhalation. There's more information to be retrieved from this data, I'm transmitting it all to you now."

Nero's advanced processor ran through the necessary calculations in less than a millisecond. "If our analysis so far is correct," he said, "this substance is the most dangerous ever created. An adult human would be dead if exposed to no more than two nanolitres of it. That phial contains 4.93 millilitres. That's enough to kill thirty-eight million people."

There was silence on the line from SWARM headquarters. At last, Queen Bee said, "So the information we intercepted last week is correct. But we still don't know if that phial is the only sample of the poison. Or how and why it was made."

"Should we remove the phial?" said Chopper.

"Should we destroy it?" said Nero.

"Negative," said Queen Bee. "Destroying it might make me feel a little safer, but since we don't know if this is all that exists, or whether more can be made easily, that might be a pointless move. We're working on the theory that this is the creation of a single rogue scientist. However, we have yet to prove that. It might be part of a larger project. Removing the phial would alert whoever knows about it to the fact that we've paid their lab a visit."

"Should I take a small amount of it for further study?" asked Sabre.

"Absolutely not," said Queen Bee. "We can't risk even an atom of that stuff getting loose. No, leave it where it is for now, safely locked away. You've accomplished your mission, and located it. We'll proceed with our original plan: Widow, you stay in the building and shadow the man we suspect. The rest, return to HQ. Good work, all of you."

CHAPTER TWO

Several hours later, two smartly dressed people joined the steady clatter of commuters going up and down the grey steps of London's Charing Cross Underground station, on the edge of Trafalgar Square. Until recently, the man had worked for MI6. The woman had been an undercover agent for the CIA. Now, they worked for SWARM.

Neither of them looked particularly remarkable, or memorable, which was exactly what they intended. Nobody around them in the crowded, echoing hall of the Underground station thought they were anything other than a couple of ordinary business people.

They rode the long escalator down into the depths of the station. The gentle clanking of the machinery beneath them reverberated off the curved ceiling above. The dusty, oily smell of the place made the woman wrinkle her nose.

They marched along with the crowd. The man checked his watch: just after 8.27 a.m. They'd be late if they didn't get a move on.

While everyone else hurried ahead, lost in their own thoughts or in the music thrumming through their earphones, the man and the woman turned a sharp left into a narrow, dimly lit passageway. Nobody took any notice of their sudden detour.

They halted at a door marked "Staff Toilet – Out of Order". The woman placed her hand against one of the wall tiles to the side of the door. Hidden inside it was a fingerprint-ID system. The tile flashed green and bleeped, and the door clicked open. With a quick glance over their shoulders to make sure they were unobserved, they went inside.

Beyond the door was an elegantly designed lift. The man spoke, apparently to the ceiling. "This is SIA agent code name J, access beta-delta-411, confirm."

"SIA agent code name K," said the woman, "access tango-alpha-924, confirm."

"Confirmed," said a recorded voice.

The lift descended rapidly. Moments later, it arrived at SWARM headquarters, part of the UK's Secret Intelligence Agency base, hidden deep beneath central London.

"Come on," said Agent J, "we should have been at the meeting five minutes ago!"

They made their way down further flights of stairs to the laboratory. It was a long, low room. Blue-tinted light came from panels in the floor. Along the centre of the lab was a line of raised workbenches. All around were display screens, machinery, files and racks of scientific equipment.

Gathered around one of the workbenches were SWARM's senior members of staff. Agent J and Agent K were SWARM's human operatives, whose job was to assist the micro-robots on their missions, if needed.

"You're late," said Beatrice Maynard. She was a tall, well dressed woman with blonde hair. Her tone of voice alone was enough to deliver a sharp telling-off.

"Sorry, Ms Maynard," said Agent K.

Simon Turing, SWARM's Data Analyst, pulled a face behind Queen Bee's back and Professor Miller, SWARM's stern Technician, frowned.

"I've called you all together," began Queen Bee, "to brief you on a very serious situation. Up until now, the details have only been known to myself and to Alfred."

SWARM's resident Programmer, Alfred Berners, took his hands out of the pockets of his cardigan. On the workbench in front of him, raised up from their resting positions inside the workbench, were the glowing, complex electronic frames in which the micro-robots were kept. The six who'd returned from their overnight mission were recharging their energy cells and listening to the briefing. Widow's frame was empty.

"A few days ago," said Queen Bee, "an email came to my attention. It had been sent by a man called Pablo Alva, from the offices of a medical research company called Smith-Neutall Bio Labs. It was sent to a terrorist in South America, a member of an underground network known as EBLS, the East Balboan Liberation Squad. Agent J, I understand you encountered this group while you were with MI6?"

"Yes," said Agent J. "East Balboa is a small republic in South America. The East Balboan Liberation Squad was formed by rebels who wanted to get rid of the brutal, corrupt dictators who run the country. For years, the EBLS was dedicated to peaceful protest, until it was taken over by hard-line revolutionaries. All they wanted was power, and they didn't care how they got it. Today, the EBLS is a terrorist organization operating in several countries. MI6 consider them a major threat."

"The EBLS are a serious danger," said Queen Bee. "So you can imagine the reaction when this email was discovered."

She touched a couple of sensors on the workbench, and a screen on the wall blinked into life. It displayed a screenshot:

FROM PAlva@SmithN.co.uk
TO   RL165423867@state.Balboa.com

New bioweapon available, created in this company's lab. Very powerful, no known antidote. Will sell it to you. Am still loyal to EBLS cause. Will contact you again soon for answer.

From the offices of Smith-Neutall Bio Labs Ltd.
This email has been scanned for all known viruses.

"Why would Alva send such a message using his own email account?" said Chopper the dragonfly, his voice coming from a speaker built into the frame surrounding him. "And from his own place of work? Wouldn't that be risky?"

"It would," said Alfred Berners, brushing a hand through his untidy white hair. "But he'd need to prove his identity to the terrorists. All sorts of data relating to IP addresses and routing servers can be mined from even the simplest email. The EBLS would need to see that the message did indeed come from someone inside Smith-Neutall, and not from, say, MI6, trying to trap them."

"Can we be sure Alva is the one who actually sent the email?" said Morph. "Couldn't it have been someone pretending to be him?"

"Access to the company's computers, including all email, is heavily encrypted, and securely recorded," said Queen Bee. "Anyone trying to break into Alva's account would show up on multiple logs and, according to Sirena's hacks from last night, nobody did."

"Why would the EBLS trust Alva?" said Nero.

"He used to be a member," said Queen Bee. "However, he broke off all contact with them after they ditched peaceful protest and turned to violence. Or so he claims."

"Do you think he was sent by the EBLS to infiltrate Smith-Neutall? To gain access to dangerous materials?" suggested Professor Miller, adjusting two pens that sat in the top pocket of his spotless white lab coat so they were precisely aligned.

"We don't know ... yet," said Queen Bee.

"What we do have is a final analysis of the chemical data collected by Sabre on last night's mission. Simon?"

Simon Turing cleared his throat and started tapping at a nearby keyboard. A long series of formulae showed on the 3D display that floated above the robots' workbench.

"Well, there's good news and bad news. The bad news is that this poison is every bit as lethal as we suspected. Nero's calculations were correct, a miniscule amount of this stuff can kill an adult human. I've never seen anything like it. You'd only have to get it on your skin to be counting your last minutes. It's an extremely powerful nerve agent, which means it mucks about with the way your body functions, but it also acts like a virus. You could put it into a spray cannister, pump it out into the air, and everyone within range would be dead as a doornail."

"What would happen to them?" asked Chopper.

"Well, if you want the gory details…" shrugged Simon. "First, you'd start bleeding all over, then your eyes would—"

SWARM

"Thank you, Simon, we get the idea," said Queen Bee. "We've only just had our breakfast. You said there was good news too?"

"Ah, yes," said Simon, raising a finger for emphasis. "This poison has a very complicated chemical structure. It is heavier than air. Which means that, although you could disperse it through the air and kill a lot of people, you can't spread it all that far. At least, not in one burst."

"Only a limited area could be affected by one attack?" said Professor Miller.

"Exactly," said Simon. "You could kill, for example, a large building's worth of people, but it wouldn't spread much beyond that. An area as big as a football pitch or two, but definitely not an entire city. To kill a large area, you'd have to keep on pumping more into the atmosphere all the time."

"But how long does it remain dangerous for?" said Alfred Berners. "Won't it contaminate an area forever, no matter how large or small?"

"No. That's the good news, part two," said Simon. "Although this stuff isn't technically alive, it still has what you might call a lifespan.

Concentrated inside the phial, it could stay dangerous for years. But let loose, it soon loses its power. Spray it over those football pitches and it'd be safe to kick off after about three days."

"So it's uniquely dangerous, but has limitations," said Queen Bee.

"It's the perfect terrorist weapon," said Agent J.

"Exactly," said Agent K with a shudder. "You can target specific people or areas, without the contamination spreading and the risk to your own life being too high."

"Now that this poison has been uncovered," said Professor Miller. "Isn't it a matter for the police, rather than SWARM? After all, if this company has developed a secret bioweapon, they've probably broken any number of national and international laws."

"Unfortunately, that's part of the mystery," said Queen Bee. "Smith-Neutall is dedicated to medical research. They develop medicines to fight diseases. The creation of a deadly poison is totally outside their normal work. That's why we're working on the theory that Pablo Alva is acting alone. He seems to have used the company's resources to follow his own research."

"So why was Alva's email picked up?" asked Agent K. "Because of his past links to EBLS?"

"No," said Queen Bee. "It was intercepted at GCHQ, the UK government's monitoring agency in Gloucestershire. It was flagged up only because of where it came from and the particular message it contained, the words it used. The fact that Pablo Alva sent it was simply the icing on the cake, as you might say."

"If this intel came from GCHQ," said Agent K, "then we're not the only ones who know about it."

"It'll be all over MI5 and MI6 too," said Agent J.

"I'm afraid so," said Queen Bee. "We're not the only ones in this race. I have a meeting at MI5 in a few minutes. I'll impress on them just how dangerous the poison is. We'll code-name it Venom. In the meantime, MI5 should be doing something useful and quietly keeping tabs on Alva's home, phone and internet use. Let's hope they do the sensible thing and leave everything else to us. This situation gives us a chance to put a stop to the EBLS's entire operation by watching every move that Alva makes. That's why Widow is at Smith-Neutall right now. It's vital that Alva doesn't get spooked and break off contact with the terrorists. We may never get a chance like this again. We watch, we gather evidence and only then do we strike. Is that clear?"

"Logged," replied the robot bugs.

CHAPTER THREE

"Pablo Alva must be arrested immediately."

A short, round man with a moustache was addressing a dozen MI5 secret agents seated around a large oval conference table. The nameplate outside the man's office said "Morris Drake – Inland Containment Officer". He stood in front of a large screen, showing a slightly blurred photograph of Pablo Alva getting into a car. Alva was thin and scruffy, with a heavily lined face and a sour expression.

"This was taken yesterday afternoon as Alva left work," said Drake. "I've had his flat and the Smith-Neutall building watched twenty-four seven. Nothing unusual has been observed. We've also been intercepting his email, both at work and at home, and the only messages that have come in or out of his account are a competition entry form, and his birthday list sent to his mum. Bless."

The MI5 agents laughed.

"So, nothing unusual there either. The internet connection into the Smith-Neutall building shows no odd or unexpected traffic, and Alva's home broadband connection has registered only a couple of hours on BBC iPlayer and a ten-minute go on Ultimate Zap-Master 4."

"What's the conclusion we draw from all this?" said Drake. "Anyone?"

The agents glanced at each other for a moment. One of them nervously raised his hand.

"That Alva's not contacted the EBLS again yet, sir. We should continue to monitor."

"Wrong!" cried Drake. "It means he must be getting his messages out some other way, and we've got to nick him right now before the EBLS launch an attack."

"What about the poison, sir?" said another agent. "That's still safely under lock and key, isn't it? I mean, they can't launch an attack without it."

"Of course they can't," said Drake. "And it's got to stay that way. That's why we must arrest Alva now, before he does the deal. He's not going to steal the poison until the last minute, is he? He's not going to keep it in a box at home! He'll snatch it and run."

The image on the screen changed. Now it showed the layout of the Smith-Neutall building.

"We need to move fast," said Drake, "because I have it on good authority that we're not the only branch of the secret service taking an interest in this. And I won't have MI6 or the SIA poking their noses into our business. Internal security is our patch, not theirs. I don't care what goes on halfway around the world, our job is to root out people like Pablo Alva on home turf. It was some secret SIA department who managed to analyze the poison, and we need to make sure they don't start taking over this operation. We all know what those top-secret weirdos are like. They'll be sending in invisible sniffer dogs or robot cleaning ladies or something!"

The agents laughed.

"And I'm not having them thinking their stupid gadgets can do our job better than us!"

The agents applauded.

"We cut off exits at Smith-Neutall here, here and here," said Drake, pointing to positions on the screen. "I want their labs secured. I want every last member of staff questioned. I want an armed guard on that poison around the clock. I want Alva in a black van and heading for the nearest interrogation room faster than you can say ... something very short. Are we clear?"

The top-floor office at Smith-Neutall Bio Labs was cool and comfortable, but the three people in it were quite the opposite. Sitting behind a large desk was Gwen Stirling, the Chief Executive, who was in charge of running the whole company. On the other side of the desk were the company's Head of Science, Dr Kirk, and the Sales Director, Peter Seede.

"The one and only positive in all this," said Gwen in a low voice, "is that nobody outside the company knows about the poison." She tapped her long fingers beside the untouched cup of coffee on her desk. Her angular nose seemed to point accusingly at the Head of Science. "You've made sure of that?"

"Oh, absolutely, Gwen," burbled Dr Kirk. He was even more tense and nervous than the others. He fiddled with his thick-framed glasses and his shoes jittered on the soft carpet beneath them. "There are only the three of us who know it exists, plus my assistants Pablo and Emma. They're both completely reliable, we can be totally sure they won't tell anyone."

"Can we?" piped up Peter Seede, the Sales Director. "Do they understand how bad things could get? If news ever leaks out that we've created this horrific stuff, nobody would ever buy any of our medicines again. We'd be shut down by the authorities and go straight to prison, thanks to your bungling!"

"We're very well aware of that, Peter," replied Gwen. "Calm down."

The Sales Director shifted uneasily in his seat, smoothing his dark hair. He tweaked at the cuffs of his expensive designer suit. "Sorry, Gwen," he said at last. "You're right, we mustn't panic. But let's be clear about who's at fault here." He threw a hostile glance at Dr Kirk.

"You know perfectly well it was an accident!" spluttered the Head of Science, shifting in his seat nervously. "An accident! We were so close to the correct formula and then the computers tracking the chemical analysis registered unexpected mutations!"

"The cold-cure formula?" asked the Chief Executive.

"Yes," said Dr Kirk. "As you know, I've been working on it for years, on and off. Finding a cure for the common cold would bring us fame and fortune. We'd have an honoured place in the history of medical science. My assistants and I were sure we were on the right track."

"And you really don't know what happened?" growled the Sales Director.

"On paper, everything worked perfectly," said Dr Kirk. "There was a mutation of the genes we spliced into the formula – something we didn't account for."

"I don't see why you can't just destroy the evil stuff right now," said Peter.

"Because we must conduct tests. We simply must!" said Dr Kirk. "We have to understand how and why our cold-cure formula went so horribly wrong. If we destroy it now, we could easily make the same mistake again."

Gwen Stirling stood up and gazed out of the window overlooking the car park. She took some deep breaths. "How long will the tests take?" she said.

"Two days," said Dr Kirk. "Maybe three."

"And once they're done, the poison can be incinerated?"

"Yes, burned away," he replied. "Every trace will be gone."

"OK," she said. "In the meantime, we stay calm and we stay quiet. Peter, we go ahead with the sales trip to Thailand as planned –" the Sales Director nodded – "We act as if nothing has happened. In a couple of days, this will all be over."

"In a few hours, this will all be over," said Drake, Inland Containment Officer of MI5, leaning closer to his communication screen. "The Smith-Neutall building will be sealed off and Pablo Alva will be in custody."

"My section is already active on this," said Queen Bee. "Storming the building would be foolish."

"Oh, would it now?" sneered Drake.

The two of them glared angrily at each other, like circling tigers fighting over territory.

"We have a perfect opportunity to end the threat from the East Balboan Liberation Squad," said Queen Bee. "If you go charging in, that opportunity will be ruined."

"My only concern is securing the poison and apprehending those responsible for it," barked Drake. "I'm not interested in any of the SIA's undercover, clever-clever game-playing."

"There are larger issues at stake here!"

Drake shook his head scornfully. "Who are

you, again, exactly? What do you do at the SIA? What's your section? Huh?"

"You know I can't tell you that," said Queen Bee.

"Exactly," spat Drake. "You lot make me sick! If Alva gets away, if that poison gets out, who'll be in the biggest trouble, eh? The section that isn't top secret, the one people know exists, my section – MI5! Headlines in the press, finger-wagging on the news, the whole works. I refuse to be bossed around! There's nothing your agents can do that mine can't."

"Really? I've heard that one before," said Queen Bee sarcastically, arching an eyebrow.

"This is my operation," growled Drake.

"I already have an undercover agent at work inside Smith-Neutall," said Queen Bee. She let Drake assume she meant a human, not a micro-robotic spider.

"So what? Back off."

The screen went blank.

Queen Bee paused for a moment to compose herself. All she would ever allow others to see of her was an iron shell of authority and determination.

However, now and again her shell would crack a little.

She stabbed at the control panel beside her. Simon Turing's face appeared on the communication screen.

"Yes, Ms Maynard?" said Simon.

Queen Bee stared into the screen. "We take action, and beat MI5 at their own game. Activate the SWARM."

"OK," said Dr Kirk, calmly, "we carry on as normal. Everything's fine, and nothing is going to happen."

His two lab assistants, Pablo Alva and Emma Barnes, glanced at each other.

"Are you sure?" said Alva. He spoke in a low voice, his East Balboan Spanish accent strong.

Smith-Neutall's Head of Science nodded. "Absolutely. I've just been speaking with the Chief Executive and the Sales Director. They're agreed that this whole terrible situation stays one hundred per cent secret."

The three of them were gathered in a corner of the laboratory at Smith-Neutall, unaware that Widow was hidden behind a nearby glass beaker, monitoring their every word. Her pointed metal legs held her motionless. Microscopic sensors pulsed across her domed abdomen.

She'd been following her orders. She had tracked Pablo Alva's movements from the moment he'd arrived that morning.

"I'm so glad nobody else knows," said Emma. "I was worried we were all going to get arrested or something."

"We continue to run our tests on it," said Dr Kirk, "and as soon as they're done, we'll destroy it and everything will be back to how it was. We've no reason to worry."

"I could hardly sleep last night," said Alva, "just knowing that stuff is around. I keep getting this terrible feeling that I'm being watched."

"Me too," said Barnes. "Guilty conscience, I guess."

"We've nothing to feel guilty about," said the Head of Science. "It was an accident. Now, I suggest we all return to work. Those tests must be done as quickly as possible."

At that moment, a signal from SWARM headquarters registered in Widow's circuits.

Her transmitter silently replied, "Widow online."

"This is Queen Bee," said the message. "Report."

"Alva arrived 8.22 a.m., went directly to lab. Made cup of coffee, talked with Lab Assistant Emma Barnes for six minutes and fourteen seconds. Do you want to hear the recording?"

"Not unless it's relevant to the mission," said Queen Bee. "Just give me a one-sentence summary."

"He's done nothing unusual today," transmitted Widow.

"Nothing at all?"

"Only standard laboratory work. Nobody has accessed the basement store. The Venom has not been touched."

Pablo was busy at the lab's desktop PC, entering figures into a spreadsheet. He paused and turned to Emma. "I feel better already, knowing that everything will be fine."

Suddenly, a loud klaxon sounded outside the

building. Alva and Barnes flinched with fright. The voice of MI5 agent Drake barked through a loudspeaker.

"This is an official announcement. The Smith-Neutall facility is surrounded by agents of Her Majesty's government. All personnel must remain where they are. All communication in and out of this building is being monitored. Do not attempt to use phones, computers or other equipment. All personnel are under arrest."

"Widow, stick close to Alva!" cried Queen Bee. "Now he knows that the authorities are on to him, he may start to delete email logs or try to get his hands on the Venom."

"Logged, Queen Bee," signalled Widow. "Further orders?"

"Stand by for updates. The SWARM is on its way."

CHAPTER FOUR

Outside, MI5 agents wearing plain clothes had ordered soldiers in body armour and helmets to form a cordon around the Smith-Neutall Bio Labs. All of them were armed with machine guns. Three army personnel carriers, their back doors wide open, blocked the entrance to the car park. Orders were shouted over the whipping sound of a helicopter positioned high above. A steady stream of soldiers and agents began to march into the building itself.

On the other side of the road, hidden behind the blinds of a vacant office block, SWARM's

SWARM

Agent J watched what was going on through binoculars. "We're way ahead of you, Drake," he muttered to himself.

He tapped a key code into a small box sitting beside him. The box sprung open to reveal the SWARM micro-robots.

Agent J spoke into his phone. "Hive 2 to SWARM."

"Acknowledged, Hive 2," said Queen Bee. "The robots' sensors show MI5's raid is beginning."

"Confirmed," said Agent J.

"Release the SWARM," said Queen Bee.

Agent J hesitated. "Are we sure about this? MI5 and those soldiers are supposed to be on our side."

"They are on our side," said Queen Bee, "but Drake has ruined any element of surprise. I don't like the idea of working against MI5 any more than you do. However, Alva will know his cover's blown. Everyone online?"

"Affirmative, Queen Bee," signalled the robots, including Widow in the laboratory.

"Our plan of action must now be updated," said Queen Bee. "To stay a step ahead of the situation, we must reverse our tactics and allow Alva to escape. Or rather, allow him to think he's escaped. He'll lead us to the terrorists. Logically, once he's on the run, he'll hook up with the EBLS in order for them to hide him."

"I can see an office window open on the second floor," said Agent J, looking through his binoculars. "Chopper, Nero, Hercules, Sabre and Morph can enter through that. Sirena can stay by the window to track movement outside."

"Throughout this raid," said Queen Bee, "those MI5 agents are to be hindered and held back, but mustn't be allowed to realize we're involved, and must not identify any robot. Is everyone clear on that?"

"Logged, Queen Bee," said the robots.

The six robots rose and darted out through the blinds, those without wings being carried by those who could fly.

"What's going on?" trembled Alva. An internal alarm chimed along the corridors of Smith-

Neutall, and a red warning light shone on the wall of the laboratory. Kirk entered, his face pale and sweating.

"It's MI5!" Pablo Alva cried. "They're sealing off the basement!"

"They must know about the poison," said Barnes.

Dr Kirk jittered with panic. "How can they possibly? I mean, how?"

Alva spun on his heels, his eyes darting all around the lab. "They can't. Unless they've got us under surveillance!"

At that moment, Widow the spider leaped from a nearby workstation and clung to Alva's back, so delicately he had no idea she was there. With lightning movements, she scuttled into his pocket in order to remain unseen. Alva began to hunt around, searching for hidden cameras and microphones.

"Don't be ridiculous!" cried Dr Kirk. "Why would anyone bug this place? It's all over now… They know!"

The other members of the SWARM signalled to Widow that they were inside the building.

"Logged," said Widow. "Mission update in effect. Alva must have access to all exits."

Meanwhile, MI5 agent Drake was in Smith-Neutall's spacious reception area. He didn't suspect for a moment that his raid was already being manipulated to suit SWARM's plans. The company's receptionist was under armed guard, frozen with fear and wondering what on earth was going on.

"Is the basement storage facility secure?" asked Drake.

"Yessir!" saluted a soldier, part of a small squad waiting for further orders.

"Good, the poison's not going anywhere. You two," barked Drake, pointing to other soldiers. "Get the Chief Executive down here now! You, you and you, join B group on the first floor and arrest Alva. Alive! The rest of you are with me."

He marched towards the nearest office. The radio clipped to the lapel of his suit crackled into life. "C group reporting. Exits sealed, sir. Phones now hacked, broadband line hacked, all staff are being held at their current locations."

Drake tapped at the radio, turning his head towards it to answer. "Acknowledged, C group."

Ahead of him, a line of soldiers was storming up a stairway. The din of their boots concealed a faint buzzing sound in the air. Sabre the mosquito flew directly above the agent at the front of the line.

"Activate plan for obstruction, allowing Alva to escape," said Sabre. He deployed a tiny, needle-like point from his mechanical mouthparts, then dived and jabbed the first agent in the neck, injecting the needle into the narrow gap between helmet and collar.

The agent suddenly jerked and let out a high-pitched yelp. He toppled backwards, sending all the soldiers behind him into an angry tangle of arms and legs.

"Freezer sting delivered," signalled Sabre calmly.

"Take care," said Chopper the dragonfly, co-ordinating data while following Drake, "or they'll realize something out of the ordinary is interfering with their operation. Hercules and Morph?"

"I'm at the main junction box," said Hercules the stag beetle. He was inside a little room, close to the reception area, where the building's electricity supply was controlled.

"Standing by," said Morph the centipede. He'd squeezed into the circuit boards behind a maintenance hatch close to Hercules.

"Nero?" signalled Chopper.

"In position," said Nero. He had crawled into the back of a PC in one of the offices upstairs. Fibre-optic probes built into his claws were tapping into the company's complex computer system.

"Go," said Chopper.

Hercules used his saw-like claw to cut through a series of cables. Sparks flew all around him. "Selected power systems disrupted," reported Hercules.

At the same moment, Morph short-circuited the board above him with his antennae. Lights switched off all over the building.

"Back-up power systems disabled," said Morph.

"Hacking into controls," signalled Nero. "I'm closing the blinds."

Window blinds shut all over the building. Most rooms and corridors were suddenly plunged into darkness. Soldiers and MI5 agents, unable to see where they were going, ploughed into walls and stumbled over each other.

A voice crackled through Drake's radio. "Power failure, sir! Someone's mucking about with the building's systems!"

"Alva!" hissed Drake angrily.

In the laboratory, Dr Kirk, the Head of Science was in a state of confused terror. "Where did the lights go? Where did the lights go?"

"Let's not panic," said Alva. "It's out of our control, we'll just have to do as the authorities say."

"We only needed a couple of days!" cried Dr Kirk. "Then it would all have been dealt with! Where's Barnes gone?"

"I don't know," said Alva, looking around. He

frowned. "She just ran out. She's been a long time, I wonder what's happened to her?"

"I'm sure she's fine. We're all going to be rounded up, anyway... We're going to prison!"

"It was an accident," said Alva. "Surely they'll understand?"

"I doubt it!" Dr Kirk said. He wavered for a moment, panic quickly overcoming his common sense. "We've got to get out of here! Maybe we can get away, before they catch us?"

Before Alva could stop him, he hurried out of the lab. The internal alarm was still sounding. Alva paused for a moment, his face a storm of uncertainty. Should he go or stay? Taking a deep breath, he followed his boss out into the corridor.

They didn't get far before hearing the sound of heavy boots thundering towards them. They came to a sudden halt. Inside Alva's pocket, Widow's sensors could detect his heart pounding with fear.

"What do we do?" whispered Alva.

Widow scuttled from her hiding place, just as half a dozen heavily armed soldiers appeared at the far end of the corridor. Through the shadowy gloom, they raced towards the two scientists.

"Stay where you are!"

The robot spider, unnoticed by the humans, shot across the floor and fired a web-line at the opposite wall. It formed a tripwire, at ankle level. The soldiers ran into it at speed, tumbling headlong.

Widow was about to race up the wall as the nearest soldier fell forward. His flailing arm caught her a hefty blow and she was knocked back, spinning in mid-air. Before she could recalibrate her sensors, she'd fallen beneath the soldier and the entire weight of the man and his body armour slammed down on top of her. His head bounced against the floor and, despite the helmet he was wearing, he was knocked out cold.

Widow's tough exoskeleton was undamaged, but three of her legs were registering as offline. She was trapped between the floor and the soldier's chest. Instantly, she transmitted a distress signal to the other robots.

"I read you, Widow," said Chopper. "Nero, see what you can do."

"I'm live," said Nero.

Back in the lab corridor, most of the other soldiers were already clambering to their feet, yelling orders at Alva and Dr Kirk to stay still. The soldiers advanced on them, their weapons and armour making them look like huge monsters in the near-darkness.

"Activating laser grid," said Nero.

There was a loud double-bleep in the corridor, and the security grid blinked into life. The soldier at the front of the group flashed out a hand, indicating for the others to halt. "Night-time defences have come on!"

"There's no way past that," whispered Dr Kirk to Alva. "Those beams will cut through steel, I installed the system myself. Come on, back the way we came!"

"You two!" shouted the nearest soldier. "Stay there!"

They were already retreating back along the corridor.

"Halt!" yelled the soldier.

He unshouldered his machine gun. Quickly, he clicked off the safety catch and raised the weapon ready to fire. He aimed, not at the scientists, but at the thin rectangle of red light that ran along the floor, walls and ceiling, marking the edges of the laser grid.

A burst of bullets tore into the walls and floor. The noise was deafening, and Alva and Dr Kirk immediately dropped to the floor and covered their heads.

The laser grid spluttered and switched off.

The soldier hoisted his gun on to his shoulder again, marched forward, and grabbed Alva by the front of his shirt. With an angry grunt, he hauled the scientist to his feet. The agent tore the Smith-Neutall ID badge from Alva's top pocket and checked it.

"Pablo Alva," he growled, "I am arresting you under the Prevention of Terrorism Act 2005, on suspicion that you are concerned in the preparation of acts of terror against citizens of the United Kingdom."

The soldier spun Alva around as if he was a bag of potatoes, and hurled him into the arms of two MI5 agents standing nearby.

The soldier who'd fallen on Widow was now staggering to his feet. Widow struggled to turn herself upright, but realized it would take her a minute or two to regain mobility. "Hive 2 to SWARM. Emergency," she signalled. "Target apprehended."

There was a three-note hum on the SWARM communications network, and Queen Bee cut in: "Widow! Can you follow them?"

"Negative, Queen Bee."

Suddenly, Widow's sensors detected Hercules the stag beetle flying low to the ground beside her. He had responded to the spider's first distress signal and rushed from the power room.

"I'm at Alva's location," he transmitted. "Should I take Widow's place?"

"Widow's data shows no suspicious activity on Alva's part, but we still don't know the truth about that email," said Queen Bee. "Until we uncover further leads, we should continue to monitor Alva. Don't conceal yourself in his clothes. MI5 will scan him and you might be found. Place a tracker egg."

"I'm live, Queen Bee," confirmed Hercules.

MI5 agents were hauling both Alva and Dr Kirk away. Dr Kirk jabbered non-stop in alarm.

Alva simply looked terrified.

Hercules, flying barely two centimetres from the floor, swiftly closed in on Alva. Adjusting his speed and direction, he landed on the back of Alva's shoe. A tiny tube shot out from the robot's thorax and stamped a microdot on to the shoe's heel. This was a miniature transmitter and listening device, designed by Professor Miller back at SWARM headquarters to be totally undetectable. Even the high-tech scanners used by MI5 and the CIA would never know it was there.

Hercules darted out of the way, and the agents dragged their prisoners out of sight. The beetle picked up Widow and carried her off. She hung awkwardly, her damaged legs twisted at odd angles.

"That's a nasty dent you've got there," said Hercules.

Widow didn't reply.

CHAPTER FIVE

Half an hour later, SWARM's Data Analyst Simon Turing and Alfred Berners, the Computer Programmer, were both tapping at keyboards. They were surrounded by the scrolling displays and high-tech machinery that filled the SWARM laboratory.

Professor Miller was sitting at a workstation in the corner, examining Widow's damaged components and making repairs. He held both hands inside a 3D-sensor array. The movements of his fingers translated into the motions of miniature tools that worked on Widow's circuits and mechanisms.

Their boss, Queen Bee, entered the room. "Ready?" she asked, walking across to Simon and Alfred. "MI5 are going to talk to Alva right now."

"Perfect timing, Ms Maynard," smiled Simon. "Alfred's broken the encryption on MI5's internal comms, so we can piggyback the signal from Hercules's tracker egg on their own frequencies. They'll never even suspect we're monitoring them."

"Excellent," said Queen Bee.

"And is Mr Drake feeling pleased with himself?" asked Alfred, peering over the top of his spectacles.

"I've heard from the top level of the SIA that he's as smug as a cat with a mouse dipped in cream," said Queen Bee. "The one thing he got right was to get the Venom tightly under lock and key. There were armed guards on that bio-storage vault within two minutes. Nobody's been inside since, and the company's computer logs show that there were no visits at all to the vault in the past two days, not since before our robots' night-time visit."

"And he has no idea we've got Alva bugged?" said Alfred.

"None," said Queen Bee.

Simon snorted with amusement. "I do love being one step ahead all the time," he said. He tapped at his keyboard. A series of tones sounded, as the SWARM computer system plugged itself into MI5's encrypted data streams. Moments later, they could hear footsteps echoing.

"They'll be taking Alva to the interrogation rooms at MI5," said Queen Bee.

"You're right," said Simon Turing, watching a nearby display. "The co-ordinates show he's on their fifth floor, close to the holding cells."

They heard scuffling, other movements, the scraping of a chair. The tiny tracking device Hercules had planted on Alva was beaming back a live audio stream, as well as his exact position. Alfred adjusted the stream to ensure that the voices sounded as clear as possible.

There was a bump, then a series of clunks and taps. Finally, MI5 agent Drake's voice came through loud and clear. Queen Bee, Simon and

SWARM

Alfred listened intently to the conversation:

Drake: Evening, Mr Alva. Glad you could join us.

Alva: You can't keep me here, I demand to see a lawyer!

Drake: Demand all you like, you ain't getting nothing. Not till we've had a nice little chat.

Alva: I know my rights!

Drake: We're not the police, Mr Alva. You're on the green surveillance list. An active suspect.

Alva: What am I supposed to have done?

Drake: Well, that's what we're here to find out. Now then, from our earlier chats with your colleagues, it seems five people knew the poison existed. Is that right?

Alva: Yes. Our Chief Executive, my boss, Dr Kirk, who's Head of Science, the company's Sales Director, me, and the other lab assistant, Emma Barnes.

Where is Emma? She disappeared.

Drake: My men caught her on her way down to the bio-storage in the basement. She claimed she was going to make sure it was securely locked. She claimed she didn't want my men blundering about in there. She claimed she was worried about the poison being taken away, or not handled correctly.

Alva: If that's what she says, then that's the truth. Emma is completely trustworthy.

Drake: That's for me to decide. My men have got her just along the corridor, until we can investigate her further. Mind you, even a brief glance at her record shows she's never been a foreign national, or a member of a terrorist organization. Looks like you're still Suspect Number One.

Alva: You don't frighten me. I left my home country to escape from bullies like you.

Drake: Let's talk about your home

country, shall we? East Balboa. Lovely countryside, I'm led to understand. Or it was, until the EBLS started blowing it up.

Alva: I'm no longer a member! I'm sure you know that perfectly well.

Drake: I know perfectly well that you claim you're not a member any more.

Alva: I have never been a terrorist. I despise violence! The reason I left the EBLS was because they started threatening people. They were an organization dedicated to peaceful protest. We wanted justice and democracy for our country. Then evil men took it over. I was horrified, I left the EBLS behind, I have a new home here in the UK, and that is all. I have no involvement with terrorists, not now, not ever!

Drake: Yes, well that's what you would say, isn't it? I mean, you're not going to come in here and say "Yes, I've been plotting to poison the world" now, are you? I mean, if you did, you'd be a pretty rubbish terrorist, wouldn't you?

Alva: If you know about the poison, you surely know it was an accident! We were working on a cure for the common cold. There were mutations in the genetic code of the serum.

Drake: It doesn't matter how it was created. It matters how you intend to use it.

Alva: I don't! Why won't you listen to me? I have nothing to hide!

Drake: Did you send an email to the EBLS last week?

Alva: What? No, of course I didn't, I told you I—

Drake: Someone did.

Alva: It wasn't me!

Drake: Someone using your email account, on your computer, at your workstation, in your lab.

Alva: What? How? It wasn't me, I tell you!

Drake: Oh dear, we seem to be going around in circles, don't we? I say you did, you say you didn't. The thing is, who's going to be believed? The ex-EBLS member who knew about this poison, who helped keep it a secret, who appears to have contacted his old terrorist buddies, who resisted arrest … or MI5? Who would you believe?

Alva: I never sent an email! I haven't been down to the bio-storage vault for days. I couldn't even tell you what the poison is being kept in!

Drake: An old yoghurt pot, I heard.

Alva: You make fun of me? That poison is deadly! If you allow even—

Drake: We know very well how deadly it is! Why do you think we raided the company in force, huh? Don't you worry, there's no way it's leaving that basement, it's safely guarded. As soon as our nerds can get in there, it'll be destroyed. Should be later today, as a matter of fact.

Alva: Good! Then this nightmare will be over.

Drake: Over? It'll be over, will it, sunshine? For you, it's just beginning.

"Turn it off," said Queen Bee. "That Drake idiot makes me cringe."

Simon Turing tapped a couple of keys and the tracker switched over to "record only".

"Alva is telling the truth," he muttered. He pointed to a series of readouts on the display beside him. "The stress patterns in his speech indicate it. Lies show up as specific changes in pitch and tone, and he's shown none."

"Yes," said Queen Bee in a low voice. "That conversation reveals three important facts. Firstly, theories about Alva have been wrong. He didn't send that email, and isn't involved with selling the Venom to the EBLS. Which means that, secondly, whoever is involved has enough technical skill to hack into Alva's account. Thirdly, SWARM's focus must now switch to the other people who knew about the Venom."

"MI5 are only interested in Alva," said Simon.

"My guess is that this Emma Barnes is now the likeliest suspect. She was heading for the bio-storage, and she'd have had the technical knowledge."

"At least if MI5 have her, we can concentrate on the final three staff," said Queen Bee. "We must stay on our toes. This situation is now completely open, anything could happen." She thought for a few moments. "Contact Chopper."

Chopper the dragonfly had taken over from Sirena on surveillance duty at Smith-Neutall. He was keeping well out of sight, darting from room to room, his highly tuned sensors and advanced eye cameras watching and recording everything.

Most of the staff had been questioned and sent home. The bio-storage was being guarded by a squadron of soldiers armed with machine guns, to ensure nobody went anywhere near it. There were more soldiers and MI5 agents on permanent patrol around the building.

The lab where Pablo Alva, Emma Barnes and Dr Kirk normally worked was filled with an array of MI5 agents, science advisers and bio-weapon experts. They were sifting through the company's records, piecing together the experiments that had accidentally led to the poison's creation.

"They'll soon be ready to destroy the Venom," reported Chopper, who was positioned above a filing cabinet in one of the offices.

"Do they have the necessary equipment?" transmitted Queen Bee.

"From what I've observed, yes," said Chopper. "MI5's science personnel are well aware of the risks. The job will be done thoroughly."

"At least that's one piece of good news," sighed Queen Bee. "I want an update on the situation there. Hack into the computers, see if you can link an employee called Emma Barnes to sending that email to the EBLS."

"Accessing now, Queen Bee," said Chopper. His circuits tapped into the probes left inside the computers by Nero. "Data is downloading… Cross-checking… Information established."

"Go ahead," said Queen Bee.

"Keystroke data shows that the email was typed and sent at time index 6:22 p.m. However, the security camera on the outside of the building shows Barnes leaving to go home, time index also 6:22 p.m. The email was written and sent at exactly the time Barnes was walking across the car park. She was not the sender."

"OK," said Queen Bee. "Check against three others: the company's Chief Executive, Gwen Stirling, Head of Science, Dr Kirk, and Sales Director, Peter Seede."

"Accessing... None are logged as being in the building at the time. However, if Alva is innocent, we know that the guilty person can interfere with the computer systems. This data is not conclusive."

"Understood. Good work, Chopper," said Queen Bee. "Where are these three suspects right now?"

"I intercepted a conversation between an MI5 agent here and MI5 HQ less than twenty minutes ago. They are accepting the claim that the Venom was an accidental creation, and are allowing our three suspects to remain free, for the time being, although under close watch. Internal sensors show that the Chief Executive, Gwen Stirling, is currently at her desk. The Sales Director, Peter Seede, has been allowed to continue with a business trip to Thailand. Dr Kirk, the Head of Science, is in the lab, assisting MI5 with their enquiries into the Venom. Can I ask a question, Queen Bee?"

"Of course." Queen Bee sounded surprised, but pleased that one of her robots was thinking for itself.

"We have proven to ourselves that Alva is innocent," said Chopper, "and that Barnes is innocent, within a matter of minutes. Of the remaining suspects, only Dr Kirk is likely to have had the technical skills needed to hack Alva's email. He's now the key suspect."

"Yes, I think you're right…"

"So, why are the humans of MI5 still questioning Mr Alva? It's not logical."

Queen Bee chuckled to herself. "You've got a lot to learn about humans."

At that moment, a tinny voice sounded around the Smith-Neutall building. "Assigned agents to basement storage vault, please. Assigned agents to bio-storage."

"They're about to destroy the Venom," said Chopper.

"Go!" said Queen Bee. "Keep a close eye on everything going on down there. Dr Kirk especially! If he's the one we want, this will be his last chance to snatch the Venom. Be prepared."

"Logged, Queen Bee."

Chopper buzzed through the building at high speed. In less than a minute, he'd made his way down through stairwells and rooms, and was on the ceiling of the area outside the storage vault.

Below him was a small gathering of agents and scientists, along with Smith-Neutall's Chief Executive. All of them were wearing yellow biohazard suits and breathing masks over their ordinary clothes. A couple of the scientists carried a large metal container, about the size of a pizza box. This was the incinerator, into which the phial of Venom would be placed and burned away. Dr Kirk held a long pair of tongs, with which he would carefully take the phial from the glass cabinet inside the vault, and deposit it into the incinerator.

Chopper took sensor readings of everything around him. Deep inside his programming, he was still puzzled by human inefficiency. His CPU began to re-analyze the many terabytes of data he'd accessed in the past couple of hours, since the raid by MI5. He wondered if there was some tiny detail that the humans hadn't accounted for so far.

And there was!

Instantly the dragonfly darted high above the heads of the scientists. He landed beside the small hole leading into the bio-storage vault, which Hercules had cut on the SWARM's visit the previous night. Folding back his mechanical wings, he quickly crawled inside, sending an emergency signal back to SWARM HQ.

"Chopper to SWARM! Gap in data detected! MI5 sealed off the bio-storage within two minutes, but sensor logs are blank for ninety-seven seconds between arrival of soldiers at the building, and arrival of soldiers down here at bio-storage!"

Chopper emerged into the pitch dark bio-storage room. His eyes switched to the green glow of night vision. He zoomed in on the glass case at the far end of the room, checking through the dozens of bottles and test tubes it contained.

"Chopper to SWARM! The phial of Venom is gone! Repeat, the phial is gone!"

At that moment, the security locks on the bio-storage vault were undone. A red light began to flash above the door. A recorded voice announced calmly, "Personnel must check protective equipment before entering. This is a biohazard area. Thank you."

There was a hiss of hydraulics. The door swung back on massive hinges. Overhead lights blinked into life inside the vault. Unseen through the scientists' cumbersome masks, Chopper buzzed back outside.

"I'm sure we're all going to feel a lot safer once this is done," said Dr Kirk, stepping into the vault, now brightly lit. There was a murmur of agreement from the others. "Thank goodness this terrible poison has been safely contained."

Back at SWARM HQ, the alarm had already been raised. Action was already being taken.

The Venom was out in the open.

CHAPTER SIX

The laboratory at SWARM HQ in London was filled with secret service technicians. Professor Miller was directing a team who were tapping into communications and CCTV systems all over the world. Simon Turing and Alfred Berners were programming SWARM's computers to intercept words, patterns or images that might provide a clue to the whereabouts of the Venom.

"It's a hive of activity in here," said Hercules.

Everyone ignored him. He and the other robots were clipped into their electronic frames, raised up from the surface of one of the long workbenches.

"That was a joke."

"Was it?" said Nero. "I'm sorry, I didn't realize."

"I'm practising my human interactions," grumbled Hercules. "They're surprisingly difficult."

"Don't bicker," said Sirena.

"We've been ordered to add our processing capabilities to the search," said Nero. "Needless talk wastes precious CPU cycles."

Queen Bee swept into the room. She held a wad of papers in one hand, her phone in the other. She marched across to Professor Miller.

"Sorry to interrupt your work, Professor," she said, "but I've got my SIA boss upstairs demanding to know what progress we've made."

The Professor gave a sharp sniff. "The Smith-Neutall building is locked down, but Chopper reports his scans show no sign of the phial there. We have monitoring in place for a radius of a hundred miles. Cameras on streets and motorways, CCTV and ticketing systems at train stations, airports, ferry terminals, every possible transport link. We're keeping a close watch on all credit card transactions and reported stolen vehicles, and adding more data sources all the time. We're still in the dark, but something has to turn up eventually."

"And in the meantime, the Venom could have changed hands fifty times and be almost anywhere," said Queen Bee.

"Since we don't yet know how that phial got out, we're broadening our net to follow as many of the company's employees as we can," said Professor Miller. He paused for a moment, watching everyone around him bustling back and forth. He drew closer to Queen Bee and dropped his voice to a whisper. "We're also following the MI5 agents who were assigned to the raid on Smith-Neutall. Given the seriousness of the situation, we have to consider the possibility that the terrorist is a traitor from our own side."

"Very wise," whispered Queen Bee. "Until we can track the phial down, our real enemy could be anyone."

Simon Turing approached them. He was clutching a bundle of documents to his chest. "Ms Maynard, I've been checking through current information on EBLS activities abroad. MI5 and

MI6 terrorist watch… There's no report of any EBLS sympathisers arriving anywhere in the UK recently."

"How does this affect the search?" said Queen Bee.

"Well," said Simon, "our terrorist will be aiming to hand the Venom over to them in person. Yes?"

"I see!" said Queen Bee. "If the EBLS isn't in the UK, then our suspect will need to travel to wherever they are."

"Right," said Simon. "We should concentrate the search on airports, and other routes out of the country."

"Good thinking," said Queen Bee. "Send Agent J and Agent K down here. And get a couple of helicopters ready." She turned to the robots. "Disengage CPUs from the mainframe computer. I want you all deployed at main international transport hubs. The SWARM can act faster and more efficiently than troops or other secret service personnel. More quietly too. There's danger of widespread panic if agents or police start marching about, and the media get to hear about the Venom."

"Whoever has the phial may be alerted too," added Hercules.

"Exactly," said Queen Bee. "I want the SWARM active, on the ground. Nero, Sirena, Morph, you'll be at Heathrow airport. We'll need three of you there because it's the biggest and busiest. We'll divert Chopper to Gatwick. Widow, Stansted. Sabre, you're at Birmingham. Hercules, the Eurostar terminal at St Pancras. Go!"

"We're live, Queen Bee!"

The cavernous halls of Heathrow airport were noisy and bustling. Passengers stared up at electronic boards, which clicked and blinked, announcing arrivals and departures. At lines of check-in desks, queues snaked back in long, controlled zigzags.

Up above, a network of fat heating pipes, electrical cables and air vents criss-crossed the ceiling. Perched on a cable, Nero the scorpion, Morph the centipede and Sirena the butterfly were hacking into the airport's data systems.

Nero's fibre-optic pincer probes stabbed into the wiring beneath them.

"I'm online with today's check-in data and operations information," said Nero.

"I've got CCTV feeds and recordings," said Morph, his antennae twitching. "Anything happening down there?"

Sirena's ultra-sensitive detection circuits were keeping a constant watch on people moving around below. Using X-ray sensors, she scanned luggage, bags and passengers. She downloaded closed-circuit camera images from Morph and used facial recognition software, cross-checked with official databases, to identify everyone who'd passed through the airport in the past twelve hours.

"Nothing suspicious," she said. "That lady down there in the blue coat has got a pair of scissors in a sewing kit in her bag. The security gate will take them from her. There's a boy with a toy sword, which will probably be confiscated too, but there's nothing that isn't routine."

"Are you monitoring physiological states?" said Nero.

"Yes," said Sirena. "Any increased heart rates, higher levels of perspiration or rapid eye movements might suggest agitation or fear. There are some nervous flyers down there, but nobody is trying to conceal their nerves, as a terrorist might. Someone carrying something as dangerous as the Venom would definitely show signs of that kind."

They both continued to watch for several minutes, motionless and in silence. Their electronic brains sorted through terabytes of data, alert to everything going on below them simultaneously.

"Approaching the Air Weihan desk!" signalled Sirena suddenly. "Face recognition is flagging up a passenger!"

"Who is it?" said Morph.

"Double-checking with SIA and MI5 databases…" said Sirena. "It's the Sales Director of Smith-Neutall, Peter Seede."

"He's already been interviewed by MI5, hasn't he?" said Nero.

"They classified him Low Risk. He doesn't have the technical or scientific knowledge to handle the Venom. We already know that his schedule shows a business trip to Thailand today. It was booked eleven weeks ago, long before the Venom was even created."

"He doesn't sound like our terrorist," said Morph.

"Scans of his luggage show nothing unusual. I would only have logged his presence, and let headquarters know we've tracked him, except for one thing – my sensors show he's very nervous indeed."

"Is he scared of flying?" said Nero.

"Accessing personnel and interview files..." said Morph. "MI5 assessed him as arrogant and ambitious, with normal intelligence. He's thirty-seven and he's worked for Smith-Neutall for six years. He complained to the Chief Executive last year about his salary, although it's well above average. He was injured in a car accident at the age of eighteen and lost part of his left hand. He isn't married, has no children, drives an Alfa Romeo, is a regular at Persephone's Italian eatery. Nothing about flying, in fact he regularly goes abroad on business."

"Let's take a closer look," said Nero.

While Sirena fluttered in a wide circle towards the check-in desk, Nero and Morph scuttled quickly along a series of cables and conduits to reach floor level.

Peter Seede was joining the back of the queue at the check-in desk. He was wearing a pristine blue business suit with a matching tie. He placed his small suitcase on the ground while he waited in line, pushing it along with his feet every time he moved forward. He looked around the concourse with an air of casual boredom, but one of his polished shoes kept up a rapid tapping against the floor tiles. Gradually, he edged closer to the front of the queue.

Nero and Morph hid under the conveyor belt beside the check-in desk. Sirena alighted on the airline logo hanging above it.

"The computers at Smith-Neutall say he's flying to a sales conference in Bangkok, Thailand," said Morph. "They also register a receipt for the cost of the air fare."

Nero made a quick check of the airport's data. "It looks like he's changed his plans at the last minute. This airline doesn't fly to Thailand. Scan his ticket."

Sirena located Seede's travel documents and passport in the inside pocket of his jacket. "That confirms it," she said. "His ticket is for Shanghai in China. A flight leaving in less than an hour."

"See if you can get closer," said Nero.

The smartly uniformed check-in attendant gave Seede a bright smile. "Good afternoon, sir, may I see your ticket and passport?" she said in a clipped Chinese accent.

Seede smiled at her and reached into his jacket.

Sirena fluttered to the lower edge of the check-in desk, from where she could scan Seede in more detail but remain hidden from view.

"Quickly," said Morph. "This may be our only chance to run a close-up check on him."

"I'll ignore the suitcase," said Sirena. "If he's got the Venom, he wouldn't leave it to get put in the aircraft's baggage hold."

"Thank you for travelling with Air Weihan, Mr Seede," said the attendant, looking at her computer terminal as she swiped his ticket through a reader. "Do you have luggage to check in today?"

"Just this one," said Seede. He placed the suitcase on the conveyor belt beneath which Nero was hiding.

"Scan active," said Sirena. "Beginning shoes… No hidden compartment…"

The attendant quickly slipped a tag around the handle of the suitcase. "Your flight is currently timetabled to depart on schedule, Mr Seede."

"That's good news."

"You've just made it in time, we're closing check-in in two minutes. You'll need to hurry!"

"Quickly!" said Morph.

"Legs, trousers…" said Sirena. "No concealed pockets… Jacket, shirt… Nothing…"

"Is there anything else I can help you with today, Mr Seede?"

"No, thank you."

"Please proceed to the security gate, and have a pleasant journey."

"Skin surface, nose, underwear…" said Sirena. "All negative."

"I'm sure I will." Seede smiled at the assistant

and walked away. His suitcase bumped out of sight on the conveyor belt.

"I'll have to risk direct contact," said Sirena. "If he's got the Venom, finding it will need a high-intensity probe."

"Be careful!" warned Nero.

Sirena landed delicately on the back of Seede's jacket. Nero and Morph kept up with them, scuttling along underneath a line of luggage trolleys. Sirena recalibrated her sensors to take readings of everything from the chemical compounds in the gel on Seede's hair to the fibres in the cotton and wool mix of his socks.

"You say he lost part of his left hand in an accident?" said Nero. "I can see his left hand from here, and it doesn't appear to be damaged."

Sirena moved to the back of Seede's left arm.

"Refocusing high-res imaging... He has a prosthetic section attached to his hand!" she said. "The last two fingers, and a small section of his palm. It's designed to look natural."

"Didn't you spot it earlier?" said Nero.

"Even now, I can only detect it at the far range of my sensors. It seems to be shielded with a fake chemical signature that reads as normal flesh. Even the most sophisticated airport or other security scanners wouldn't pick it up... There's a shape lodged inside his little finger! The missing phial! He's carrying the Venom!"

CHAPTER SEVEN

Seede suddenly swatted at his left arm and frowned at the butterfly that had brushed past him.

"I've been seen!" transmitted Sirena. "Withdrawing to safe distance!"

"Send a full report to SWARM headquarters," said Nero. "Morph and I will stay with him."

At that moment, a female voice echoed through the airport concourse. "Last call for Flight AW91 Air Weihan to Shaghai, boarding at Gate 12. Last call for Flight AW91."

Peter Seede walked calmly but quickly over to

the security checkpoint. A sour-faced guard ran an electronic wand around him, then ushered him into the arched X-ray detector. No alarms were triggered and the guard motioned for Seede to continue on to the gate.

Nero and Morph followed, scuttling along the corridor. Morph kept to the thinly carpeted floor, while Nero moved along the high ceiling, the two of them staying apart in case one of them was spotted as Sirena had been.

"Once Seede is on the aircraft," said Nero, "SWARM headquarters should be able to stop it leaving by raising an official alert. Seede will be trapped and the police can arrest him. Until then, we must keep track of his movements."

They shadowed Seede into the departure lounge. It was almost empty, as most of the passengers had already boarded the flight. The Air Weihan jet, a huge Boeing 767-300, could be seen through the enormous windows that formed one wall of the lounge. A steward was stationed at the metal tunnel which led out to the plane, hurrying the last few passengers through and collecting up their boarding passes with a weary smile. He beckoned to Seede.

"Should we follow him on to the aircraft?" said Morph.

"It shouldn't be necessary," said Nero. "He won't be able to escape once he's aboard."

"I'll signal headquarters," said Morph.

Moments later, Queen Bee cut in on the robots' communications network. "Nero! Morph! How long before that flight takes off?"

"Eight minutes until the plane proceeds to the runway for take-off," transmitted Nero.

Queen Bee muttered something under her breath, then said, "We can't get the plane grounded quickly enough. There are too many phone calls to be made. We can't use Sirena's scans without... Anyway, it's complicated. The only agents who can act in time are you two. You must stop that aircraft from taking off."

"The airport authorities would respond instantly to a bomb threat," said Nero. "Could SWARM pretend that—?"

"Absolutely not," interrupted Queen Bee. "We do not resort to such irresponsible tactics. It's our duty to protect this country!"

"Apologies, Queen Bee," said Nero. "I was considering the problem logically."

"As you're programmed to do, it's fine. Our actions against MI5 during their raid on Smith-Neutall broke the rules, but we must draw the line at actions that are morally wrong."

"Understood," said Nero.

"I have been computing alternatives," said Morph. "The only way for Nero and I to prevent the aeroplane taking off is to damage its systems, or at least trigger alerts in the cockpit that would cause the pilots to delay the flight."

"We'll have to sneak on board after all," said Nero.

"Make sure that plane doesn't leave, especially with you on it!" said Queen Bee. "SWARM is classified above top secret in the UK. In China, the discovery of micro-robots like you would be considered as hostile espionage, or even as an act of war! The political consequences could be catastrophic. Sabotage of that plane is the only option. Get moving, time is short! Queen Bee out."

Without a moment's hesitation, Nero and

Morph hurried along the metal tunnel linking the gate to the aircraft. The tunnel was filled with cold air, heavy with the smell of fuel. The 767's engines were already whining into life, gradually getting louder as the rotors speeded up.

The robots, keeping well out of sight, reached the point where the tunnel met the curved outer surface of the plane. The last passengers were being hurried on board.

"My scans show the most effective sabotage would be to the flight guidance controls," signalled Nero. "There's an access panel close to the flight deck."

The robots crossed the small gap between tunnel edge and aircraft. Inside, they clung to the ceiling. The microscopic electro-claws built into the ends of their legs allowed them to move along swiftly.

The sound of the engines rose higher. Flight attendants bustled around each other in the confined space of the crew area. There was a steady chatter of voices as passengers took their seats and settled down for the long flight.

Nero and Morph reached the bulkhead that

sealed off the flight deck from the rest of the aircraft. At floor level were a series of grilles and panels.

"Third panel," said Nero. "Locate the circuit board marked 'B2' and disable it."

Morph flattened his body and squeezed through at the panel's edge. "It's locked with a key," he said. "An electronic lock would be no problem, but an old-fashioned, five-lever mechanism will take time."

A scratchy voice sounded over the plane's tannoy. "Cabin crew to doors and cross-check."

A female flight attendant swung the plane's entrance door shut and sealed it with a twist of a lever. The sound of the engines was suddenly muffled.

"Hurry!" said Morph. "Get in here, I need you to unscrew this plating."

"Working on it," said Nero. His pincers struggled to loosen the panel. Hercules would have been able to slice through it in seconds, but Nero's pincers were designed for more delicate tasks. He didn't have the strength to force the panel open, and neither did Morph.

"I can't reach SWARM HQ," said Morph. "The signal's not getting through."

"These aircraft have systems designed to stop outside electronic interference getting in," said Nero. "Those systems are now also blocking our signals from getting out."

The aircraft began to vibrate slightly. The power of the engines was increasing. Further orders crackled over the tannoy. The 767 gave a judder as it began to reverse away from the airport terminal.

"Quickly!" said Morph. "If we don't stop the plane taking off, our mission has failed."

Nero gave a sharp pull and at last the panel opened. Morph scurried out. Behind the panel was a metal plate, held in place with four tiny screws. A screwdriver head flipped out of Nero's pincer and the first screw was undone with a lightning-fast whirr. It dropped on to the carpeted floor.

"Three to go!" said Morph. "We have only seconds left!"

The aircraft taxied towards Runway 2. In the cockpit, the pilots and navigator were talking to the airport's air traffic controllers.

The second screw was undone. Nero worked as fast as he could.

"Quick!" said Morph. "Two left!"

The aircraft moved smoothly out on to the runway, turning at the end of the three and a half thousand metre concrete strip to face its take-off position. The cabin crew finished demonstrating emergency procedures to the passengers, and strapped themselves in. The "Fasten Seatbelts" signs shone red. The engines rose to a roar.

The last two screws fell and the metal plate dropped away. Morph scuttled inside the panel, scanning rapidly for the B2 circuit board.

The pull of the aircraft suddenly increased. The passengers felt themselves pushed back in their seats. The 767 sped faster and faster along the runway.

"Just a few seconds," said Morph. "Circuits located!"

"We're too late!" cried Nero. "We're taking off. If we interfere with the systems now, we'll place the humans on board in danger. Remember what Queen Bee said."

"You're right," said Morph. He scuttled out and Nero closed the panel. "What should we do? If we hurry, we can still leave the aircraft before it takes off, through the landing-gear bay."

"Our mission has failed," said Nero. "We are out of contact with HQ. We must think for ourselves. We need to devise a new mission. I think we need to stick close to Seede and the Venom."

"Despite the possible risk of causing a war if we're detected?" said Morph.

"None of the risks we'll face are greater than the risk of the Venom being released," said Nero.

"Agreed," said Morph. "This is a dangerous situation."

The 767 accelerated to take-off speed.

Nero and Morph were completely on their own, until they could re-establish contact with SWARM. Despite their mechanical components and electronic brains, they now understood what it must be like for a human to feel afraid.

CHAPTER EIGHT

"What?" gasped Queen Bee.

"The security systems on board aircraft like that are very efficient," said Professor Miller. "Nero and Morph won't be able to signal us, and we can't signal them. Not until they get off that plane."

"What about through an internet connection?" said Simon Turing. "Aircraft are online."

"All web traffic is routed through a single, managed server," said Alfred Berners. "Communications would be detected. We'd risk our robots being discovered."

"Then they're truly on their own, for the first time," said Queen Bee.

The eleven-hour flight to Shanghai was uneventful. Nero and Morph hid beneath passenger seats close to where Seede was sitting. They monitored his every move.

He dozed for a while, ate two spoonfuls of the meal that was served to the passengers while the aircraft flew over the Caspian Sea, and listened to the in-flight radio. He complained to a woman behind him several times about her little boy, who kept kicking the back of his seat, and complained to an air steward about the snoring of a man a few rows behind him.

Nero and Morph remained motionless throughout the journey, silently recording everything Seede did. Morph noted that Seede's heart rate stayed slightly higher than normal, indicating his nervousness. The fingers of his right hand tapped constantly at the arm rest beside him, while his left hand, with its prosthetic section, was mostly kept pushed into the pocket of his jacket. He flicked through a magazine plucked from the seat-back pocket in front of him, and he flicked between the in-flight radio and movie channels, but generally he was too preoccupied with his own thoughts to do anything other than restlessly wait...

At long last, the captain's voice crackled from the tannoy again. "Ladies and gentlemen, we will soon be commencing our descent into Shanghai Pudong International Airport. Local time is 12.55 p.m. and local weather conditions are cloudy but pleasantly warm at twenty-one degrees Celsius. On behalf of the crew, I'd like to thank you for travelling Air Weihan today, and wish you a pleasant onward journey."

The aircraft took another half an hour to finally glide into place at the airport terminal. Passengers gathered their things, stretching and grumbling after the long flight. Nero and Morph stayed put until the first rush was over, then quickly hitched a ride on Seede as he joined the shuffling line of people leaving the plane. Morph slid into his top pocket. Nero snipped a tiny hole in the lining of Seede's jacket and wriggled through, staying close to the hem where he was least likely to be noticed.

As soon as the micro-robots were off the plane, Nero signalled SWARM HQ back in London. He transmitted an update on the situation.

"We're all glad to hear from you again," said Queen Bee. "You made the right choice. Stick close to Seede."

"Logged, Queen Bee," said Nero.

Seede went through Passport Control, retrieved his suitcase from the long, mechanical carousels in the arrivals hall, and walked out of the airport's main entrance. He hailed a green and grey taxi.

"Zhongshan Qi Street," he said, "just off The Bund."

The driver gave a nod, and said something that couldn't be made out through the chewing of his bubble gum. The taxi sped away, taking Yan'an West Road on to the elevated motorway leading into Shanghai's smog-shrouded city centre. As the car reached the bank of the huge, swirling Huangpu River, it turned left. It passed modern hotels, and old buildings left over from the days when the city had been under European control. Across the water stood the elegantly shaped skyscrapers of Shaghai's futuristic skyline, dominated by the Oriental Pearl Tower.

The taxi came to a halt outside a line of upmarket shops. Seede paid the driver in yuan, the local currency, and headed down a side street.

Seede paused for a moment outside a traditionally styled cafe. Its open front showed an interior painted red and black, with bulbous red lanterns hanging from the ceiling, and small tables where chattering people crowded around bowls of steaming food. A few tourists were dotted among the locals. Seede ignored the short queue at the serving counter, and weaved his way around the diners to a table near the back. Seated there were a man and a woman, both wearing sunglasses and hiking boots, with backpacks hanging on their chairs. They looked like tourists.

The man was short, stocky and greying at the temples, with a heavy moustache. The woman was taller and more stylish, her long ginger hair swirled into a large bun at the back of her head. Both were picking at a serving of noodles with wooden chopsticks. Seede sat down beside them.

The man leaned closer to him and spoke with a Spanish accent. From his hiding place in the lining of Seede's jacket, Nero transmitted the conversation back to London. In SWARM's lab, Simon Turing recorded it.

"Identify yourself," said the man, in a voice laced with suspicion and threat.

"My name is Peter Seede. I first contacted you by hacking the email account of Pablo Alva. We've been corresponding via encrypted message boards to negotiate this meeting and a price for the merchandise. Do I need to go on?"

The man sat back a little. He glanced around the cafe. Everyone was intent on their food and their chatter. From the kitchens came the sound of clanking pots and voices barking orders in the local dialect.

"OK," said the man with a grim smile. "My friend here will scan you for bugs. I'm sure you understand. Even a trusted associate can be working for the cops."

Seede nodded amiably. "Of course."

Nero sent an urgent message. "Morph! They'll detect us! Temporary shutdown, thirty seconds!"

"Logged."

The two micro-robots powered down a split second before the woman activated an app on her smartphone. She watched a stream of numbers form a graph on the screen. Nero and Morph's advanced exoskeletons reflected a signal that registered only as non-organic material containing no electrical charge.

"He's clean," said the woman. Her accent was eastern European.

When the SWARM robots rebooted, they heard Seede asking the two strangers for their names. The man said he was called Hernandez, the woman Vinski. Morph's analysis of their voice patterns indicated that they were both lying. Seede's heart was racing, although he was making great efforts to appear calm.

"Where is Pablo Alva now?" said Vinski. "Is he aware of your actions?"

"No, you needn't worry about him," said

SWARM

Seede. "He's completely in the dark."

Hernandez's chair creaked as he shifted his weight. "To business, then? You have the merchandise?"

"By the skin of my teeth, yes," said Seede. "MI5 raided the company, and I had only a couple of minutes before the place was locked down. All I had time to do was erase evidence of my visit to the vault where the stuff was kept."

"How have you accomplished all this?" said Vinski. "I thought you weren't a scientist?"

"I'm not," said Seede. "Everyone back home thinks I have no technical knowledge at all. But I've done a great deal of private study. I know more than enough, thanks. It got me the goods."

"It's hidden elsewhere, I take it, or my friend's scan would have shown it up."

"Hidden, yes," smiled Seede. "You have the money?"

Hernandez nodded. "Give us the details of the account into which you want it paid, and my friend will transfer the money as soon as you give us the merchandise."

Seede had the numbers and access codes

relating to a secret Swiss bank account printed out on a slip of paper. His nerves momentarily blanked his memory of where he'd put it.

In the top pocket of his jacket, the folded piece of paper lay wedged just beside Morph's head.

Seede rummaged through his other pockets.

Morph flattened his exoskeleton, pulling himself as tightly as possible into the bottom corner. He tucked his legs and antennae into the thin lining of fluff that had accumulated in the seams beneath him.

Seede's fingers suddenly dived into the top pocket. They moved left and right, feeling for the paper. Morph sensed a slight brush against his side. If he delved any deeper, Seede would find the micro-robot.

With a lightning movement, Morph flicked his head against the folded paper. It was knocked into the path of Seede's fingers. Seede nipped it tightly and plucked it out of his pocket.

"Ah, I knew I had it somewhere," he smiled, pushing the slip across the table. Vinski picked it up and switched her smartphone to an online banking connection.

"The payment is as agreed," said Hernandez. "Five million pounds sterling. We will wait here while you retrieve the merchandise."

Seede grinned at them. "I'm afraid not. Payment first."

Hernandez and Vinski glanced suspiciously at each other. "What?" said Vinski.

"You'll get what you're paying for, when you've paid for it," said Seede. Morph registered a sudden increase in his heart rate and perspiration.

Hernandez shifted in his chair again. His voice dropped to a sinister growl. "That is not the way it works, my friend. You've never dealt with us before, so we will give you the benefit of the doubt. We are reasonable people. Business people. As are you, yes? The goods, please. Now."

Seede stared levelly at them, his expression as blank as he could make it. He'd spent much of the flight to Shanghai mentally preparing for this moment.

"Only I know where it is. Without me, you'll never get your grubby little hands on it. Isn't that right?"

Hernandez's eyes narrowed. Vinski's gaze

flicked between Hernandez and Seede.

"The price has doubled," said Seede. "I want ten million. Or I walk away right now."

Hernandez's voice became a sibilant whisper. "You walk out of here, and you'll be dead before you reach the corner of the street. We have twelve men watching this cafe."

"If I'm dead, you'll never find the goods," said Seede quietly. "Trust me. The price is ten million. I can never return, you understand. MI5 would trace me in the end. Not that I'd want to go back. I plan to disappear, to set myself up on some lovely warm island somewhere. That sort of thing doesn't come cheap."

"The deal is five million," growled Hernandez.

"Ten," said Seede. "Not. One. Penny. Less. You know the goods are worth it. More, even."

Hernandez paused for a moment, then suddenly smiled and shook his head. "Now, my friend," he laughed, "I have seen the true face of greed."

Seede laughed too.

Hernandez snorted amusement, then became serious again. "And what is to stop us killing you the minute you hand over the merchandise?" he said. "If you think you're going to rip us off, you are sadly mistaken."

"Ah, but I've come prepared," said Seede. "You've brought your heavies with you, I've brought mine. Hired assassins, ready to wipe you out, and anyone else in your organization they can track down, if I don't reach my lovely warm island. I can afford them, now."

In Seede's top pocket, Morph's sensors showed that Seede was lying too. He was calling Hernandez's bluff.

Hernandez turned to Vinski. "Pay the man," he grunted.

Seede couldn't stop himself grinning with triumph. Vinski tapped at her smartphone. A few seconds later, she turned the screen around to show Seede the payment confirmation. Seede consulted his own phone to double check that the money was in his account.

"Thank you," he said.

He leaned forward across the table, extending his left hand, palm upwards. "By the way," he said, "what do you plan to do with it?"

"It's no concern of yours," muttered Hernandez.

"Just curious," shrugged Seede. "I don't want to find that the lovely warm island I choose is right in your firing line, that's all."

"We have a carefully devised plan," smiled Vinski. "The company which created the merchandise will be bombed. That way, those who created it will die, the records of it will be destroyed, and the possibility of an antidote being developed will be reduced. Then, one week from now, the merchandise will be let loose in two locations. The United Nations building in New York, and the EU headquarters in Brussels. Neither of which are lovely warm islands."

"I see," said Seede. "There are major governmental meetings in both cities that day. Maximum chaos. I expect half the world's leaders will be killed."

"The world will not be able to act," said Vinski, "when the EBLS stages revolutions in neighbouring South American countries, and then further afield."

While she spoke, Seede took hold of the little

finger of his left hand. He gave it a sharp twist, then slowly pulled it away, leaving behind a tiny pair of plastic clips. Then, holding the fake finger by its tip, he unscrewed a small lid at its base and slid the phial of Venom out. He very carefully placed it on the table in front of Hernandez.

"You had it here in front of us all the time!" laughed Hernandez. "My friend, I take my hat off to you. You have outwitted the EBLS at every turn, it seems."

A series of loud clangs came from the kitchen, followed by angry cries. The cafe's cashier, perched on a stool close to the street, was arguing with an American over his bill. The diners and tourists paid no attention to any of it, and carried on eating and talking.

Vinski pointed to the hollow finger, amazed. "You created this just to transport the goods to us?"

"Actually, I've had it for quite a while," said Seede. He didn't tell her that he'd used it several times in the past, to sell the company's secret formulas to foreign rivals.

Vinski scanned the phial using an app on her

phone. The results caused her face to pale. "The specs he sent us were correct," she muttered, a tremble in her voice. "This is so toxic it's off the scale."

Seede clipped the fake finger back on to his hand, and stood up.

"Nice to do business with you," he said. "Goodbye."

"*Adios*," smiled Hernandez.

Seede picked his way around the tables and back out into the street.

Hernandez whispered to Vinski, "I placed a guy at the airport. Seede arrived alone. Too tight to really buy protection, I guess. Not so clever after all." He pointed to her smartphone. "Make sure someone hacks his account, gets the money back."

Outside, Nero and Morph got ready to leave Seede's jacket. "Nero to SWARM," said Nero. "Confirm pursuit."

"Confirmed," said Queen Bee. "Track the phial, leave Seede. We can deal with him later."

The robots slipped away from Seede as stealthily as they had hitched a lift on him. They dropped to the pavement and quickly moved into the gutter, where they were less likely to be spotted.

Neither of them detected any unusual activity in the street. The armed EBLS terrorist on the roof of a nearby block of flats was too far away to alert their sensors. He ended his phone call from Hernandez and took aim with his automatic rifle.

Three loud cracks echoed along the street. People paused in alarm, looking around for the source of the noise.

Seede halted in mid-step. For several seconds, he stood motionless. He looked down. Three circular red stains were growing across his white cotton shirt. His shoulders slumped, his knees buckled, and he pitched forward, landing with a smack on his face. He was dead before he hit the ground.

"Leave him," said Nero. "He's not our concern any more."

People in the cafe were either trying to see what was going on in the street, or else getting up and rushing outside. The robots hurried over to the table near the back, where Seede had been sitting.

Hernandez and Vinski were gone. So was the Venom.

CHAPTER NINE

"Scan!" said Nero.

"The kitchen area shows two more humans than were there a minute ago," said Morph. "They must be escaping through the back of the cafe."

The robots scuttled at high speed into the kitchen. They were just in time to see Hernandez and Vinski leaving through a back door.

Three cooks in heavily stained chef's whites were too busy arguing with each other and attending to their sizzling pans to care what else was going on around them. The robots hurried through the pot-clanking, steam-filled kitchen and emerged into a dark, narrow alleyway. Walls dotted with lichen rose high on both sides.

Hernandez and Vinski were approaching a people carrier parked at the far end of the alley. Nero and Morph caught up with them as the terrorists climbed inside. Hernandez snapped orders in Chinese to a man in the driving seat.

The car pulled away at speed. The robots were clinging tightly to the mud-splashed rear wheel arch, the tyre spinning just centimetres below them. The rumbling roar of the car's tyres against the road echoed around them. It was beginning to shower with rain. Water droplets sprayed off the wheels.

"My internal energy cells are running a little low," transmitted Morph.

"Mine too," said Nero. "We must watch out for opportunities to recharge. We don't know how long we'll need to track these terrorists."

"Logically," said Morph, "the terrorists will put their plans into operation immediately. Any delay increases their risk of being caught."

"They'll need to place small quantities of the Venom into explosives, or some kind of aerosol device," said Nero. "That will require specialized equipment and knowledge. I think Hernandez and Vinski will now head directly to find such facilities."

"That could be many places in the world," said Morph.

Nero made several million calculations of probability. Then he signalled SWARM HQ.

"The other robots confirm your mathematical analysis," said Simon Turing, in the lab. "Because we now know that their first target is Smith-Neutall, a return to London is the most likely outcome. The EBLS will want to have as few members involved in the operation as possible, to further reduce the risk of capture. Therefore, Hernandez and Vinski themselves are likely to be the ones who'll blow up Smith-Neutall, then weaponize the Venom. Then they'll split up to place devices in New York and Brussels."

"Correct so far," transmitted Morph. "We're arriving back at the airport now."

Queen Bee's voice cut into the communication channel. "Don't worry about being out of contact again. We trust your judgement. SWARM are making preparations here. Our plan will be put into action the moment you re-enter UK airspace. We'll close comms for now."

"Logged, Queen Bee," said Nero and Morph.

As the car pulled into a passenger drop-off bay, the robots descended to the ground. Hernandez and Vinski got out. The robots watched the terrorists' feet go around to the back of the vehicle, and heard the clunk and wheeze of the rear hatch lifting. Two small travelling cases were unloaded.

"Time to hitch another ride," signalled Nero.

Morph scurried rapidly to the back of one of the knee-high boots Vinski was wearing. He flattened himself against the leather, so that he would appear to be nothing more than a curling design on the boot's surface. Nero slipped into one of the dusty turn-ups at the bottom of Hernandez's heavy black jeans.

"Wait! I can't detect the Venom," said Morph. "They must be carrying it in something that blocks scans, like Seede did. If only we had Sirena's high-res sensors here! Could the Venom be hidden in their luggage?"

"Unlikely," said Nero. "Just like Seede, they'll want to keep it with them. The luggage will be part of their disguise as tourists."

The terrorists checked into Air Weihan's next flight back to the UK. The robots powered down while Hernandez and Vinski went through security, to make sure they weren't detected, then rebooted while the terrorists waited in the departure lounge. Vinski flicked through a technology magazine, while Hernandez stood watching aircraft come and go.

Unlike Seede, the terrorists travelled in the First Class section, towards the front of the plane, screened off from the other passengers. Of the ten seats in First Class, and thirty in Business Class, only half were occupied.

"They're making sure they're noticed by as few people as possible," said Morph.

As soon as the flight had taken off, and the "Fasten Seatbelts" sign had gone out, Hernandez and Vinski both tipped their plush seats back into a reclined position. Vinski squeezed off her boots and let them bump on to the thick carpet. Morph crawled under the seats, and Nero joined him in the shadows. The springs of Hernandez's seat squeaked above them as he settled down for a nap.

Using his pincers, Nero snipped three sides of a square into the carpet, and flipped up the resulting flap to reveal a small access port for the aircraft's electrical system. "We can tap into the power grid from here, and recharge."

The robots sent tiny fibre-optic probes into the access port. They soaked up power to bring their internal energy cells back up to maximum.

On the flight deck, the pilot and co-pilot sat in front of a wide dashboard covered in instruments, dials, readouts and switches. Above the complex array of controls, sunshine could be seen reflecting off the tops of the clouds at 30,000 feet above the ground.

The co-pilot noticed a fluctuation in the power grid. He spoke into the microphone attached to his headphones. "Mike, I'm reading a small tap on the electrical system. Definitely not plug sockets, passenger Wi-Fi or our own equipment."

"Whereabouts?" asked the pilot.

"Somewhere among the passengers," said

the co-pilot. "Can't pinpoint the exact spot. It's probably nothing, but I heard London had a security issue earlier today, so..."

"You're right, I'll put the cabin crew on alert, get them to run a discreet search. Storage lockers, under seats, that sort of thing. Some sort of hidden device may be operating, maybe data gathering. Probably just a glitch, but better safe than sorry. If there's trouble brewing we should find it, before it finds us. Call a flight attendant in here, will you?"

CHAPTER TEN

With the minimum of movement, Vinski nudged Hernandez awake. He blinked and grunted at her for a moment. With her eyes, she pointed over his shoulder. Frowning, he slowly turned around, trying to make it appear he was having a yawn and a stretch.

A female flight attendant was making her way slowly along the aisles of the First Class section. She was opening the overhead storage compartments as quietly as possible, peeping inside, then clicking them shut again. She kept stooping to peer under seats and between them.

She smiled warmly at anyone who gave her a funny look, and asked them if they'd like anything to drink.

Hernandez leaned close to Vinski and whispered. "What's she looking for?"

"I've no idea. Maybe someone just lost something?"

"Then why be so secretive about it? Why not ask?" whispered Hernandez. "I don't like this. Something doesn't feel right." The flight attendant was now carefully and casually sorting through a rack of newspapers and magazines at the front of the cabin.

Beneath Vinski's seat, the two micro-robots had also noted the flight attendant's odd behaviour. "It looks as if she's searching for us," said Morph, "but how does she know we're here?"

"Their suspicions must have been raised somehow. Perhaps our recharge registered on the electrical systems," said Nero. "They may incorrectly suspect some kind of sabotage."

"We can't stay here, then," said Morph. "She'll see us as soon as she looks under the seat."

"We'll hide in Vinski's boots," said Nero.

The robots took cover inside one of the boots, which still lay discarded on the cabin floor. By now, the flight attendant had finished searching the magazine rack, and was progressing down the aisle towards Hernandez and Vinski. Hernandez kept a close watch on her. She drew level with him, her attention fixed on the area around the empty seats behind him.

"Can I help you, miss?" he said with a smile.

The flight attendant suddenly snapped upright. "Oh no, thank you. It's fine."

"Have you lost something?"

"Umm, yes. A passenger on an earlier flight left their, er, contact lens case behind."

Hernandez flashed a meaningful glance at Vinski. In whispers, they had been weighing up the possibility that their plans had been discovered by the authorities. They had also discussed options, in case their cover was blown and they had a fight on their hands. They decided they'd take one or more of the cabin crew hostage; they would hijack the flight and divert it. The look the two terrorists exchanged was filled with unspoken messages.

The flight attendant was a little flustered. "All a bit embarrassing. For the airline, you understand. We like our passengers to—"

"Here, let us help you," smiled Hernandez.

Hernandez and Vinski made a show of pulling their seats upright and looking around on the floor.

"Oh no, really, thank you," twittered the flight attendant, "I don't want to put you out, I'll be—"

Vinski twisted around to get a better look at the area beside her seat, touching at her bun as she moved her head. Her feet swung to one side, and she accidentally kicked her boots. They were batted aside, hitting the metal supports of Hernandez's seat with a clatter.

Before they could react, both Morph and Nero were knocked out into the open. Morph instantly wriggled flat into the carpet and disappeared into the gap Nero had cut under Hernandez's seat.

Nero landed on his back. He had to flip his body over before he could scuttle away. His mathematical brain knew immediately that he was very likely to be spotted.

"What's that?" cried one of the passengers. "Is it a scorpion?"

"A scorpion?" echoed the woman he was travelling with.

The First Class section was suddenly filled with voices. Passengers who had been dozing, reading or watching movies all scrambled to get to their feet.

"Please remain seated, ladies and gentlemen," called the flight attendant. "I'm sure it wasn't, er, anything to worry about."

"Are you joking?" piped up the passenger who'd seen Nero first. "That was a scorpion! They can be deadly, you know!"

Nero had scurried for one of the air-ventilation ducts, located at floor level around the edge of the cabin. He ducked inside, safely hidden from view.

"Nero," signalled Morph, "stay put. I've monitored the flight deck's avionics, and we're currently heading west over Norway. It should only be a few minutes before we're in UK airspace. SWARM will be on their way then."

"Have your sensors picked up where the

terrorists are hiding the Venom yet?"

"Negative," said Morph. "It's well shielded, wherever it is."

"I'll stay as close to the terrorists as possible," said Nero.

"Logged," said Morph.

Nero recalibrated his eyes and looked out into the cabin, between the thin metal slats of the ventilation duct. The flight attendant had managed to calm the passengers. However, all of them were sitting in their seats as if they expected to get an electric shock at any moment. Hernandez and Vinski seemed nervous for the first time. Nero's analysis of their movements showed that they were jittery and uncertain.

The micro-robot considered the current mission status: the Venom was still hidden, the aircraft's crew suspected sabotage, and now every pair of eyes on board was looking for what they thought was a dangerous scorpion. Not an ideal situation.

At SWARM headquarters beneath the streets of London, the 3D display in the laboratory glowed into life. Data Analyst Simon Turing and Professor Miller, SWARM's Chief Technician, both looked up sharply from what they were doing.

A stream of data and graphics appeared on the screen.

"The aircraft is sixty-four kilometres off the coast of Norfolk," said Simon. "It's about to enter the area run by Heathrow air traffic control at Swanwick."

"I'll call Ms Maynard," said Professor Miller.

Within a minute, Queen Bee was in the laboratory. "Those EBLS operatives could do any number of things, if they think they're cornered," she said. "We have to treat the situation aboard that aircraft as the highest level of emergency. Current status of our human agents?"

"Agent K is already in the air, piloting the stealth jet," said Professor Miller. "The remaining SWARM robots are with her, active and online. Agent J is at Heathrow."

"Agent K is twenty-two kilometres from the Chinese aircraft," added Simon. "She's ready to use the experimental G-Launch device."

"Excellent," said Queen Bee. "Remain on alert. Looks like action will be taken within minutes!"

"This is Flight AW92 Air Weihan to London Heathrow, come in LHR."

On board the plane, the pilot spoke calmly and clearly into his headset. He adjusted controls on the flight-deck dashboard in front of him.

"Swanwick tower, acknowledge that, AW92," buzzed the reply from the airport's air traffic control centre.

"ETA at outer marker is seventeen minutes," said the pilot. "AW92 out."

He turned to the flight attendant, who was standing behind him.

"Well?" he demanded. "Have you caught that thing yet?"

The flight attendant paused for a moment. "No. Sorry, Captain. We've got every member of the cabin crew on it, I assure you."

The pilot growled with frustration. "Do you

have any idea how bad it would look if one of our passengers got bitten? We'd lose our jobs, you can be sure of that!"

"Stung," said the flight attendant quickly.

"What?"

"Stung, Captain. Scorpions don't actually bite."

"Oh, get out! Find that insect!"

In First Class, Nero was keeping watch on Hernandez and Vinski, who in turn were keeping watch on the aircraft's crew, who were searching the cabin from top to bottom. One of them was questioning Vinski about the "scorpion". Had she known it was there? Had she brought it on board the flight? How did it get inside her boot? Was she playing some sort of prank?

Nero could tell that Vinski was very irritated by this attention, but the terrorist continued to smile politely. She protested that she had no idea how anything of that kind could have happened.

Hernandez was becoming more anxious by the minute. He kept glancing up and down the cabin, reacting to every movement.

"Where are you, Morph?" signalled Nero.

"I've crawled up into one of the overhead

lockers," said Morph.

"I think I may have to render Hernandez unconscious, with a sting from my tail," said Nero. "He's losing his nerve. When humans become agitated, their ability to think clearly is impaired. Everyone on this aircraft could be in danger."

"Be careful," said Morph. "I'm continuing to scan for the Venom. Any clues you can give me would be welcome."

"Logged," said Nero.

Meanwhile, Hernandez shooed the flight attendants away and spoke quietly to Vinski. "If these idiots think you've deliberately brought a dangerous animal on board, we'll both be detained at Heathrow. We cannot put our fake identities at risk. I'm going to collect our insurance."

He stood up and walked away down the aisle towards the Business Class and Economy Class sections. Nero dashed out of the ventilation duct.

"Morph, it sounds like they've hidden the Venom somewhere else in the plane," he signalled. "Hernandez may be fetching it now. I'm going to disable him."

The robot scuttled rapidly underneath the line

of seats beside the cabin's port-hole windows. He overtook Hernandez, and zipped across the floor. He aimed directly for the terrorist's right ankle.

Suddenly, Nero's motion sensors and vision circuits registered a flash of movement. He was trapped, surrounded by glass.

"Got it!" cried one of the First Class passengers. "Look, it's a scorpion all right! I saw it crawling under those seats, so I got ready to pounce!"

The others craned their necks to see. Nero had been caught under a large upturned glass. The passengers cheered with relief, and gave a round of applause. The nearest flight attendant bustled over, gushing congratulations.

"Well done, sir! I'll tell the captain at once. And I'll fetch something to hold that pesky little so-and-so in until we land."

Nero's claws and tail were dotted with drips of the lemonade which the glass had contained. He could easily have thrown the glass aside, or cut a hole in it, but no real scorpion could have done that. To maintain secrecy, the SWARM robots had to look and act like real insects. With many unauthorized humans gawping at him, Nero had to maintain his cover.

Meanwhile, Hernandez had entered the toilet cubicle at the rear of the First Class section. In the dull glow of the overhead light, he crouched down beside the tiny wash basin. He pushed at a rectangular panel at its base.

The panel gave way. He reached far inside, searching along the water pipe with his fingers. At last he found what he was looking for, and wrenched it free of the sticky tape which was holding it in place. Earlier that day, he'd arranged for his contact at Shaghai airport to do two things. The first was to monitor Seede when he arrived from London. The second was to disguise himself as one of the airport's maintenance crew and secretly place this item on Flight AW92, for Hernandez to retrieve if needed.

Hernandez withdrew his hand. In it was a fully loaded gun.

CHAPTER ELEVEN

SWARM's Agent K was at the controls of a stealth fighter jet, designed to be invisible to radar, infrared and other detection systems. The fighter's dark, angular shape swooped through the cloud cover five hundred metres behind Air Weihan Flight AW92.

Agent K pulled the fighter up to within twenty metres of the huge airliner, flying precisely underneath its tail. A complex display of information shone across the visor of her flight helmet. It blinked as she activated a control beside her right shoulder, and a target sight appeared in the centre of her vision.

"Ready to deploy G-Launch," she said into the microphone suspended in front of her.

"Fire when ready," said Queen Bee at SWARM headquarters.

Agent K flipped open a cover to reveal a tiny joystick. She clicked it and it bleeped into life. On the nose of the fighter, a squat, barrel-like nozzle suddenly appeared. The target sights on Agent K's helmet display shifted as she moved the joystick with her thumb.

She took careful aim, then tapped the end of the joystick. The nozzle fired a large, dark blue ball. With a wet thump, it hit the closed bay doors on the underbelly of the 767, behind which were tucked the aircraft's landing gear. The ball stuck fast to the metal skin of the plane, warped by the impact into an upside-down dome shape.

"Queen Bee to SWARM, get moving."

"We're live, Queen Bee," signalled Chopper the dragonfly. "Sensors and power levels are at maximum."

Chopper, Widow, Hercules, Sabre and Sirena

were all contained inside the blue blob.

"Hercules, get us inside," said Chopper.

The stag beetle cut into the plane's metal skin, using his serrated claw. Within seconds he'd made a neat, exact circular hole, 1.2 centimetres in diameter.

"The gel around us will dissolve in less than five minutes," said Chopper. "Let's go."

The five micro-robots climbed through the tiny hole one by one.

"We'll work our way through the electrical and air circulation systems. Come in, Morph and Nero, what is your current status?"

"Online! As humans would say, it's great to hear from you!" signalled Morph from the First Class section. "I'm concealed in the overhead lockers. Nero has been moved to the cabin crew's area, between First and Business Class, and placed in a sealed plastic tub. He's being watched and cannot act. Vinski is still in her seat. Hernandez is now returning from the toilet cubicle. Wait, scanning… He has a hand gun in an inside pocket, fully loaded, database check identifies it as a Smith & Wesson Model 645."

Hernandez walked back to his seat with an arrogant swagger. He sat down and gave Vinski a brief smile.

"If we're left alone," he whispered, "then I'll put our insurance back where I found it before we land. Otherwise, get ready. We'll aim to divert this plane halfway across Europe, get it to fly at low altitude, then escape using the emergency parachutes from our luggage in the cargo hold. We can lay low until our people get to us."

Vinski gave him a curt nod, but Morph's sensors could tell she was even more agitated than he was. Her feet patted nervously against the floor.

Now that Nero had been caught, only Hernandez and Vinski were on the alert. Nobody noticed five miniature robots sneak into the cabin. Chopper, Hercules and Sabre got in through the same ventilation ducts that Nero had used. Widow and Sirena emerged from an electrical conduit behind a microwave oven in the cabin crew's area.

"Do we know the location of the Venom yet?" signalled Chopper.

"Negative," said Morph.

"We must proceed with extreme caution until we know where the Venom is," said Chopper to the SWARM. "The lives of millions of people could be at stake. Sirena, see if you can get close enough to Vinski for a high-res scan."

"Logged," said Sirena.

"Nero, are you OK?" said Chopper.

The robot scorpion looked around the see-through plastic lunch box in which he was being held. "I think I understand the human concept of embarrassment," he said. He scuttled back and forth for a few moments, to divert the attention of the two nearby flight attendants. Widow zipped behind them on a web line, and Sirena fluttered past, while they were wrinkling their noses at Nero.

"Eugh, horrible thing, isn't it?"

"If only I had feelings, they'd be hurt," transmitted Nero.

Meanwhile, Hernandez had reclined his seat again. He handed Vinski a magazine.

"Act normal," he whispered. "I think the fuss may be over."

Vinski looked over his shoulder. The female flight attendant who'd first gone looking for Nero was approaching them. "No, it isn't," she whispered.

"Excuse me, madam," smiled the flight attendant. "I just wanted to let you know that the authorities at Heathrow will need a quick word with you upon our arrival."

"Why?" said Vinski, her nerves showing in her voice.

"Oh, it's just routine, nothing to worry about. But if something like that scorpion turns up on a flight, we have to notify them. The UK has very strict quarantine regulations. The scorpion's species will have to be identified. They'll just want to ask you about where you went in China, that sort of thing. Completely routine."

"That won't be possible," said Hernandez. "We have an urgent appointment in London."

"It will only take a few minutes, sir, I'm sure," smiled the flight attendant. "Just routine."

"We had nothing to do with that creature

being on this aircraft," said Hernandez. "Perhaps I should complain to the airline about insect infestation?"

"There's no need to adopt that tone, sir," said the flight attendant, suddenly no longer smiling. "These regulations are for the benefit of everyone. I can involve Airport Security if you'd rather, sir. The scorpion was in the lady's footwear, and I know it's unlikely that—"

Her words ended in a gasp. The click of the gun's safety catch sounded centimetres from her nose.

"Shut up," said Hernandez quietly.

He jumped to his feet and grabbed her by the collar of her uniform. The other passengers suddenly noticed what was going on.

The cabin was filled with screams. Several passengers stood up.

Hernandez levelled the gun at them. "Out to the back! All of you! This aircraft is under the control of the East Balboan Liberation Squad! If anyone presses the alarm, our prisoner dies!"

The passenger who'd trapped Nero turned to the others. "He's bluffing! You can't get a real gun on a plane!"

Without a moment's hesitation, Hernandez aimed the gun at the passenger's leg and fired. The bullet skimmed the back of the man's calf. He yelled in pain and dropped to the floor.

More screams filled the air. Confusion broke out. The passengers scrambled in their panic to get away. The injured man followed, limping and swearing, a patch of blood showing on his trousers.

Vinski joined Hernandez at the front of the First Class section. Her boots were back on. Her fingers fluttered nervously at the side of her head, tapping at her swirl of hair.

Meanwhile, Chopper calmly signalled the SWARM. "Switch to attack mode. Prepare to neutralize targets."

"The Venom!" said Morph suddenly. "It's hidden inside Vinski's hair!"

"You've scanned it?" said Chopper.

"No. No time to explain now," said Morph.

"Hercules, retrieve it immediately!"

Hercules flew at top speed along the side of the cabin, swinging around to approach Vinski from the side.

Hernandez pressed the gun to the flight attendant's head. "We're going on a detour," he hissed.

Sabre the mosquito buzzed close to the ceiling. "I'll sting both terrorists now!"

"Wait," said Chopper. "Not while that human female is in danger. We cannot risk her being harmed. Remember Queen Bee's orders."

Hernandez manhandled the flight attendant over to the entrance to the flight deck. He pressed the barrel of the gun against her cheekbone. "Enter your code. Get us inside."

Hercules dived into Vinski's tightly wound ball of hair, his claw set to fire a low-powered laser beam. The terrorist was too focused on Hernandez and the flight attendant to notice the micro-robot.

"There's a network of wires in here," signalled Hercules. He quickly sliced through a series of looped cords. "Her real hair is being used to cover it. It's designed to deflect scans or detection beams, rather like Agent K's fighter jet deflects radar. Very impressive. No wonder we couldn't find it." He crawled through the gap he'd cut.

"My sensors have detected the Venom!" said Sirena. "Now that Hercules has disrupted the network around it, I can see it's contained in a small black tube, similar to the hollow finger Seede used."

Hernandez gave the flight attendant a shake. "The code!"

"Morph," signalled Chopper, "warn the pilots."

"I'm already on my way," said Morph the centipede. He was at the lower edge of the flight-deck door. He flattened his flexible exoskeleton down to less than a millimetre and wriggled through the door's curved rubber seals.

Hernandez whispered to the flight attendant. "You have to the count of five, and then you're dead... One..."

Morph emerged on to the flight deck. He was now inside the physical and electronic barriers which prevented remote takeovers of the aircraft's controls. Immediately, he transmitted a message to the earphones of the pilot and co-pilot.

"Two..." said Hernandez.

"This is a representative of the British secret

service. Your flight attendant is being held hostage by terrorists, and you must not open the door. Please continue on to London Heathrow as planned. The situation will be under control soon."

"Three…"

"Where the devil is that coming from?" spluttered the pilot.

"Inside this cockpit, according to the readout," said the co-pilot.

"Don't be ridiculous, man, there's only you and me in here!"

Meanwhile, Hercules flew clear of Vinski, the black tube containing the Venom clutched tightly beneath him. "Target acquired," he said.

"Four…"

Hernandez levelled the gun against the flight attendant's temple. In a split second, Chopper calculated the odds of eighteen different courses of action. He opted for a simple, direct approach to the problem.

The dragonfly shot across the cabin, increasing the speed of his wings so that they produced a loud, droning buzz. He dived at Hernandez.

The terrorist got a flashing glimpse of something coming at him. He started in surprise.

Chopper sent an overload command to his eyes. A dazzling flare of light suddenly burst less than a metre from Hernandez's face. The terrorist cried out in alarm, his vision suddenly a blank wash of white. He almost dropped the gun.

As Vinski stepped forward to grab the weapon, Sabre the mosquito darted at her. Before she could reach for the gun, he injected a microscopic pellet into her neck.

She jerked back, a wild expression on her face. Hernandez staggered, still blinded.

The flight attendant seized her chance. She knocked the gun out of Hernandez's hand, then ran out of the First Class section, the same way the passengers had gone.

Vinski stood like a statue for a moment, then toppled over. "Freezer sting delivered," said Sabre.

Hernandez, blinking and shaking his head, let out a yell of anger and scooped up the gun. He began to follow the flight attendant. Widow the spider leaped up from the floor. She fired a steel-strength web around the terrorist's hand, pulling it tight as she arced over his head. The gun fired, the bullet hitting one of the window seats and causing an explosion of stuffing.

Widow swung rapidly around her prey, binding him tighter and tighter from shoulders to ankles. He struggled uselessly, finally losing his balance and falling into a squirming heap beside the motionless Vinski.

"Venom recovered. Terrorists neutralized," said Chopper calmly. "Time for us to leave."

The SWARM robots quickly disarmed the fallen gun, and vanished from the scene. Nero was alone in the cabin crew's area, now that the crew had joined the passengers hiding in the Economy Class section. He flipped the lid off the plastic lunch box he was trapped in, and followed them.

Air Weihan Flight AW92 continued on to Heathrow, landing only four minutes after its scheduled arrival time. The passengers and cabin crew, huddled fearfully in Ecomony Class, cheered loudly as the aircraft taxied towards the airport terminal.

As soon as the plane's door was opened, a

small squadron of SIA officers came on board, led by Agent J. They found Vinski in a state of temporary paralysis, and Hernandez trussed up with what looked like a long length of thin wire. The remaining bullets from his gun had gone. The pilot and co-pilot were frantically searching the flight deck for the source of the message they'd heard.

Meanwhile, the SWARM robots quietly left the plane through the tiny hole Hercules had made earlier. They dropped to the tarmac below, where SWARM's Agent K was waiting to transport them back to London.

Late that night, the staff and robots of SWARM were assembled in the laboratory at SWARM headquarters. Queen Bee ran through the mission, pointing out where improvements to procedures or equipment could be made.

"There is one thing I'm still puzzled about," said Alfred Berners. "I programmed the robots' brains, and Simon Turing constructed their databases, yet Morph made a leap of logic on that return flight which I would never have expected."

"Yes," said Simon. "Completely out of the blue. It shows the robots are learning all the time; they're developing their own ways of thinking."

The robots were gathered on the lab's central workbench. 3D displays flicked and scrolled around them.

"What do you mean?" said Morph, his voice relayed through speakers hidden in the flat surface beside him.

"How did you work out that the Venom was inside Vinski's hairdo?" said Alfred.

"Humans instinctively protect what they value," said Morph. "The Venom was of enormous value to the terrorists. I thought that Vinski's raising of her fingers to her hair was nothing more than a nervous gesture at first. But she did it more than once during the flight, and I realized that she was unconsciously protecting her hiding place."

"You see?" said Simon with a beaming smile. "Intuitive reasoning!"

"What about Pablo Alva?" said Chopper.

"MI5 have let him go," said Queen Bee. "They're extremely embarrassed about the whole incident. He's said he'll go to the papers if they start threatening the staff at Smith-Neutall with prosecution. I think they'll let sleeping dogs lie. Agent Drake is looking especially red-faced. And I think Smith-Neutall will be more careful about who they employ as sales people in future."

"And the Venom?" asked Professor Miller.

"You needn't worry on that score," said Queen Bee. "I saw it incinerated myself."

She crossed to the screen on the wall, and tapped her debriefing notes shut.

"Well done, everyone," she said. "Another successful mission."

At the same moment, less than twenty miles away, two men met in the shadows of a derelict house. One was Drake of MI5. The other was a gaunt, slightly stooping man, with heavily lidded eyes and a permanently downturned mouth. They regarded each other with caution for a minute or two.

"You have it?" said the gaunt man. His voice sounded unnaturally loud in the stillness of the night.

Drake took a small, oval case from his pocket. "Safe and sound. The technical guys say you'd need a bomb to break this open. The contents are totally secure."

He handed it over. The gaunt man turned it round in his long fingers, gazing at it thoughtfully. "Amazing, isn't it?" he said. "Something as small as that, capable of such destruction. MI5 and the SIA think it's destroyed?"

"Oh yes," grinned Drake. "Got one over on them there. We burned up a fake phial. They think Venom is a thing of the past."

"Good," the other man replied. "Some branches of the secret service don't know a useful tool when they see one, eh? Your payment will be made tonight."

Drake nodded. Both men went their separate ways.

CHAPTER ONE

"Queen Bee to agents! Prepare to move out!"

Two electronic voices replied, one after the other. "I'm live, Queen Bee."

Queen Bee sat in a high-backed black leather chair, in front of a wide bank of brightly lit screens and readouts. She was a tall woman with a shock of blonde hair and a smartly cut suit. She wore a pair of glasses with small, circular lenses that reflected the rapidly shifting light from the screens. Behind the lenses, her steely grey eyes darted from one readout to another, soaking up information. Her age was difficult to work out from her looks, but her slightly pursed lips, and the way her long fingers tapped slowly on the arms of her chair, showed that she meant business.

One of the screens in front of her showed a man coming out of an office block. Numbers and graphs danced across the lower part of the image, sensor readings of everything from the air temperature at his location to his current heart rate.

Queen Bee leaned forward and spoke into a microphone, which jutted out on a long, flexible stalk. "Chopper, begin data recording."

"Logged, Queen Bee," said one of the electronic voices. It had a slightly lower tone than the other one.

Outside the office block, Marcus Oliphant sniffed at the morning breeze for a moment. He was a tall, stringy man with bushy eyebrows and a loping walk. His nose wrinkled. The smell of vehicle exhaust seemed stronger than usual today. He took a tighter grip of the small metal case he was carrying, then set off along the street. The traffic of central London rumbled and roared past.

A long set of black-painted railings ran alongside him. He didn't notice two insects perched on top. One was a tiny mosquito, the other a large, iridescent dragonfly. At least, that's what they appeared to be. They didn't jump and flit like insects usually do. Instead, they seemed to be watching him.

As he walked off down the road, the insects' wings buzzed into life, and they rose into the air, following him at a short distance.

As the insects rose, so the image on the screen in front of Queen Bee shifted and moved.

Queen Bee swung around in her chair. Sitting behind her were half a dozen people with serious, quizzical expressions on their faces. Among them were the Home Secretary, the head of MI5 and Queen Bee's boss, the leader of the UK's Secret Intelligence Agency.

"As you can see, ladies and gentlemen," said

Queen Bee, "the subject has no idea that he's being tailed. Our micro-robots are much more effective than normal secret service agents, with their blindingly obvious dark glasses and their suspiciously unmarked fast cars."

The head of MI5 shuffled grumpily in his seat. "And much more expensive. How much are these technological toy soldiers costing, Home Secretary? You gave the SIA the go-ahead for this programme."

The Home Secretary looked slightly uncomfortable. "A lot. I'm afraid I don't have the figures to hand," she muttered.

"The latest technology is never cheap," said Queen Bee. "But my section, the Department of Micro-robotic Intelligence, has capabilities that make it priceless. The existence of SWARM is known only to my staff, and to the people in this room. However, nanotechnology is the future. Micro-robots will soon dominate the worlds of spying and crime investigation. These SWARM operatives are the most advanced robots on Earth. On the outside, they are almost indistinguishable from real insects, yet each has equipment and capabilities that make the average undercover agent look like a caveman."

The Home Secretary pointed to the screen. "Who is that man? What's this demonstration supposed to prove?"

"He's Marcus Oliphant, leader of the team that's developed the new Whiplash weapon," said Queen Bee. "It has been created by a private company, Techna-Stik International, and is being sold to the British government. The prototype is in that metal case there – it's only the size of a matchbox. He's on his way to meet with your own officials, Home Secretary, and show them the progress that's been made. I've asked for my robots to shadow him today, to show their effectiveness. Normally, an MI5 operative would be assigned, but since Whiplash is every bit as secret as SWARM, this man's visit has been judged low risk. No unauthorized person could possibly know what he's carrying."

"Whiplash?" said the Home Secretary. "Have I been briefed on that?" She turned to the man beside her.

"It's an EMP device," said the head of MI5.

"Extremely dangerous in the wrong hands."

"Extremely dangerous even in the right hands," muttered Queen Bee.

"EMP?" frowned the Home Secretary.

"Electro-magnetic pulse," explained Queen Bee. "It emits an invisible wave of energy which knocks out all electrical circuits. Fries them beyond repair. It does almost no physical damage, but destroys electronics – everything from air-traffic control to TV remotes. Vehicles, computers, the lot, all made useless."

"Whiplash shoots a narrow EMP beam across a few kilometres," said the head of MI5. "It's designed to target and disable enemy systems."

Suddenly, the high electronic voice of the mosquito cut across the air. "Sabre to Queen Bee. Suspicious activity detected."

READ THEM ALL

OUT JANUARY 2015:

SIMON CHESHIRE

Simon is the award-winning author of the
Saxby Smart and *Jeremy Brown* series.
Simon's ultimate dream is to go the moon,
but in the meantime, he lives in Warwick
with his wife and children. He writes in a
tiny room, not much bigger than a wardrobe,
which is crammed with books, pieces of
paper and empty chocolate bar wrappers.
His hobbies include fixing old computers
and wishing he had more hobbies.

www.simoncheshire.co.uk